MAYA

My Miscarriage Angel

JESIE D. JOBSON

BALBOA.PRESS
A DIVISION OF HAY HOUSE

Balboa Press books may be ordered through booksellers or by contacting:

Balboa Press
A Division of Hay House
1663 Liberty Drive
Bloomington, IN 47403
www.balboapress.com
844-682-1282

Because of the dynamic nature of the Internet, any web addresses or links contained in this book may have changed since publication and may no longer be valid. The views expressed in this work are solely those of the author and do not necessarily reflect the views of the publisher, and the publisher hereby disclaims any responsibility for them.

The author of this book does not dispense medical advice or prescribe the use of any technique as a form of treatment for physical, emotional, or medical problems without the advice of a physician, either directly or indirectly. The intent of the author is only to offer information of a general nature to help you in your quest for emotional and spiritual well-being. In the event you use any of the information in this book for yourself, which is your constitutional right, the author and the publisher assume no responsibility for your actions.

Any people depicted in stock imagery provided by Getty Images are models, and such images are being used for illustrative purposes only. Certain stock imagery © Getty Images.

Print information available on the last page.

ISBN: 979-8-7652-2570-7 (sc)
ISBN: 979-8-7652-2571-4 (hc)
ISBN: 979-8-7652-2572-1 (e)

Library of Congress Control Number: 2022903709

Balboa Press rev. date: 04/13/2022

I dedicate this book to all the mothers who have lost their children. May my story remind you of the spirits and love for your babies that are now your guardian angels.

ACKNOWLEDGMENTS

First and foremost, I want to thank my children for introducing me to my connection to the world beyond ours. Thank you for holding my hand as I embarked on this spiritual journey. You are my first dreams and desires and have made this life so magically sweet to live. Being your Momma is one of my greatest blessings.

To the Father of my children, I couldn't have lived this beautiful part of my life without you, your love, and your support. This book wouldn't have been possible without your undeniable support. May this book be a celebration of our love and remembrance of our time here on earth together.

To my Aunty Donna, there aren't words to describe my gratitude for all your help in shaping me as not only a writer but a powerful woman. Your willingness to do what you love gave me the courage and pathed the way for me to know I could write books too. Thank you for the endless hours and support you spent helping me build this dream of mine. You were always the first person in my mind when I felt like I needed help. Thank you endlessly for so many beautiful gifts.

To Azure, thank you for the three years that completely changed my life financially. Joining you on your determined path to success enabled me to fund my dreams. May you always know how many lives you improve just by being the true you.

To the entire team at Balboa Press, thank you for helping shape my dream into reality. This book has been molded with care, concern, and the knowledge of many people. For this, I am forever grateful.

Love Always,
Jesie Danyelle Jobson

CHAPTER 1

ASK AND IT'S GIVEN

Danyella couldn't believe her eyes. She had seen it a million times in her mind, but there it was right in front of her, and she knew she had created it. Her thoughts flashed to the countless hours she had spent mentally constructing every detail of the house she was standing in. The awareness of her power was almost more thrilling than standing in her dream house itself.

She scanned the empty living room in awe. The details had always been slightly fuzzy in her mind mostly because her desires changed daily, but she was enjoying the deliciousness of reality's clarity. The floor-to-ceiling windows that lined the large room really did make the living room and kitchen feel grand, just as she had intended. She slid her hands across the large marble island that spanned almost the entire length of the kitchen and faced the fireplace on the opposite wall of the living room. It would be the perfect place to line barstools for their informal meals and cheerful company as she cooked and baked.

"It's no mansion, but it has the open concept that you are looking for," Danyella's realtor, Ron, said, breaking up her string of thoughts.

"It's perfect," she replied.

"Is this a real fireplace?" she asked, while inspecting the glass door opening under the stone mantel.

"It sure is. Hard to find these days in newer homes. You have to check out this deck and pool," Ron said, his voice trailing off into the backyard.

Danyella didn't need to see it. She already knew what it looked like. In fact, she knew what the whole house looked like. She had spent many hours fantasizing this exact house into existence. "This is the one, Ron!" she said confidently as she followed him to the backyard.

"That was too easy. You haven't even seen the best part yet!" Ron said, obviously determined to show her the rest of the house. "Over here, Danyella! Come see my favorite part of this property. I love this part so much that if you don't buy it, I will!" He walked to a corner of the backyard. Danyella trailed leisurely behind him while scanning the cozy outdoor space.

Ron motioned in a Vanna White fashion at the brick wall that lined the backyard and was covered in dark-green ivy. Danyella snickered because she knew what lay behind the seemingly plain brick wall. She wanted to savor this moment because she knew Ron was about to reveal something she had always dreamed of since she was a child.

"Looks like a nice wall," Danyella teased playfully.

"Exactly!" Ron said sounding like a game show host in the winning round. "But you're wrong!" Ron swept aside an armful of

2

green ivy as if he were pulling a stage curtain aside to reveal a door. Even after he started to open the unseen door, the frame barely became visible. "Come into your secret garden," Ron said.

Danyella ducked under the small willow tree branches that arched over the doorway as her ears instantly caught the soft sound of a water feature trickling in the corner. She closed her eyes to absorb the tranquility of the peaceful space, which felt like they had walked into a scene from an enchanting movie.

"It's a little overgrown and obviously needs some tending to, but I'm sure you wouldn't mind taking care of that, would you, Danyella?" Ron said with a wink.

"Oh my gosh, Ron! My kids will never get me out of my garden now." She giggled while surveying the garden. She walked around the green space, touching plants with enthusiasm. To anyone else, it was just a silly garden, but to Danyella, it was proof that magic really existed. If she could build a secret garden in her mind and have it turn up in the backyard of her dream house, she knew that the opportunities to bring things into her reality were endless.

"When I found out about this garden, I knew that this was the house for you, Danyella. It reminded me of the feeling I got when I helped you and John buy your first home several years ago!" Ron exclaimed.

It was more perfect for Danyella than Ron could have known.

As they toured the rest of the house, Danyella secretly savored each moment by taking in the fullness of every detail that her mind had always left out. She delighted in how many perfectly placed built-in shelves the house had, a detail she clearly desired but one that she didn't remember consciously constructing. As they walked up the stairs to the second floor, she noticed the wainscoting on the wall of the staircase. She also had never fully developed that detail in her daydreams, but it was perfect. She smiled as she relished each new discovery. She couldn't wait to share her news with her aunt Samantha. What a peak in energy she had experienced. She smiled, feeling the sureness in her creation. The words of her wise teacher floated to the surface of her mind: "It is as easy to build a castle as it is to build a button." This castle felt as small as a button compared to the beautiful things Danyella had already built.

Ten Years Earlier

Danyella knelt quietly in the small chapel. The light streaming in through the stained glass windows and from the single can light above the altar barely made the two rows behind her visible. As she knelt in the dark room on a prie-dieu, she stared at the statue of a bloody Jesus hanging on a cross.

She wasn't religious. She didn't follow the man-made rules of organized religion. She often referred to herself as freely spiritual. She had been raised by a Christian father and an atheist mother. Growing up with the opposing beliefs of her divorced parents, Danyella found a beautiful middle ground. She felt the realness of what most people called God, the universe, source, or any other religious name. She felt a separation from being labeled a sinner, as well as referring to this God energy as a father who only accepted followers but had the ability to accept them all. The rules seemed backward to her.

At a young age, Danyella decided on her own that her God was named Love and that Love didn't have any rules. Love wasn't her father or mother. Love was not picking sides or judging people for the way they lived. Love was present in her happiest moments and seemed so far away in her angriest. Love seemed to be a part of her. Love was the strongest part of her and everyone else.

Danyella's unique belief system seemed to make her a religious chameleon. Growing up, she had attended church services with friends and family of many faiths from Catholic to Baptist and Mormon. She found their services similar in basic structure; they usually all had some form of lecture followed by singing and prayer and usually ended with some formal or informal snack and drink. She found it best to focus on the things she enjoyed while tuning out the parts that seemed destructive. She always favored the grandmas who served the coffee and cookies at the refreshment tables, the emotional songs everyone sang, and the extended-family feel that all congregations had.

Staring at the statue of Jesus on her lunch break at the Catholic hospital she worked for, Danyella began to pray as instructed by the religious congregations she had learned from throughout her life. At first, she wanted to beg for a child, but she knew that Love had already heard her many cries for a baby over the last year. The Sunday morning lectures she had heard as a child reminded her that when Love wasn't providing something she asked for, it must be something different from what she needed.

"Please, Love ..." Her voice sounded quaky and oversized in the lonely room. "Please give me patience." Her throat filled with emotion at the thought of waiting any longer for something she had desired almost her whole life. Her impatience felt overbearing. "I know I don't do this praying thing very much. I'm not sure if I'm even doing this right." She exhaled deeply at the hilarity of criticizing herself in a prayer. That was something she had obviously inadvertently picked up from one of the organized religions' stringent rules. "I ... I just want to have patience and faith that my baby will join me on earth in perfect timing." Tears slid out the sides of her eyes and down her narrow cheeks and melted into her pinched lips. As soon as she prayed for patience, she felt a sting of fear that her request was beckoning a long treacherous journey. She sat in silence for what seemed to be an appropriate amount of time to end her request. "Thank you, Love. Amen," she said while wiping tears from her almond eyes and pushing her blond hair from her flushed face. She took a deep breath and cleared her sinuses to hide any sign of emotion before opening the door to the world outside the lonely chapel.

Walking back through the office halls to her cubicle, she felt different but could not pinpoint why. She felt that something had been set in motion. The hospital business office was unusually quiet; it lacked its normal afternoon bustle. It reminded Danyella of the calm before a storm.

"Danyella!" Shawn, her manager, shouted. He rushed toward her at an unusually brisk pace. His face shone a shade of nervous pink.

"Hi, Shawn. On your way to a meeting?" she asked playfully. Her calm voice and carefree demeanor seemed to heighten his nervousness.

"Yes I am. And with you actually. Can you meet me and Deb in the conference room in five minutes?" he rattled quickly without slowing down for her reply.

"Yes of course," she said, beginning to blush herself; she turned into her cubicle. She still wasn't used to all the pressure and overwhelming number of meetings she had to attend due to her recent promotion to department supervisor. She had received her new title just the past week, and she was in training for her new role. Shawn's sudden rush for unplanned meetings wasn't out of the ordinary, but Danyella thought he was a little more frazzled than usual. She shrugged off the heightened sense of intuition and gathered a pen and paper.

Walking into the conference room, she felt the air fill with an undeniable tension. Deb, her department director, was standing on the other side of the oversized conference table with her permanent smile and hands clasped like a professional statue. Shawn was fidgeting with a pen and smiling uncomfortably at Danyella. She scanned their faces for clues as to what might be going on. The awkward tension encouraged her to quickly take the seat nearest to the door.

In a low, automated tone, Deb said, "We're so sorry, but we're forced to retract the supervisor position due to having overlooked a major hiring detail."

Deb's perfectly placed pause made Danyella realize that Deb had done this several times before. She felt her heart quicken, and her ears began to ring. *Are they serious?* she wondered. She looked back and forth between Shawn and Deb as if they could hear her silent cries and sense her panic.

"We hope you'll stay with us in your previous position," Deb said as she awkwardly moved papers around the table.

Who would want to stay? Danyella wanted to scream. Instead, the flush of shock on her face was the only emotion she allowed to escape. She was a skilled artist in people pleasing, and like a knee-jerk reaction, she began to hold back any emotions hoping to make this uncomfortable situation less so.

Deb's instructions sounded like muffled white noise humming in Danyella's ears as her eyes slowly began to appear dreary and filled with tears. She tilted her head forward hoping that her long blond hair would curtain the flush that was flaming her fair face.

As instructed, she signed on the dotted line, matched their fake smiles, and said softly, "I wish the best to the next candidate. Thank you very much for hiring me for the supervisor position. I'm grateful for the opportunity."

They all knew her opportunity had been very short-lived—just a few days in fact. She stood, shook their hands, and politely exited the painful room. She quickly walked past an office full of curious coworkers avoiding making eye contact with anyone. Everyone in the office knew the unspoken rule; any employee entering the conference room with Deb and Shawn never left with a smile. The thudding sound of her racing heart seemed to overtake her focus as she nervously grabbed her coat and keys and escaped from the office full of people. Mustering every ounce of energy required, she kept her composure until she reached the haven of the empty elevator. With the clamp of the metal doors, her tears broke free. Sobbing alone, Danyella heard a soft voice in her mind say, *Everything happens for a reason.* Taken aback by the advice of an independent inner voice, she paused her stream of depressing thoughts. The pause made space for a moment of emotional relief. The elevator doors slid open to the bustling first-floor lobby. Her reality set back in, along with a strong urge to cry.

When she got home, her intuition urged her to her bathroom cabinet. Her puffy eyes scanned the organized toiletries while her mind searched for the reason she was staring into the dark cabinet. *What am I looking for?* Blaming it on her emotional exhaustion, she ended her search. But before she closed the cabinet door, her eyes fell on a stack of unused pregnancy tests. Memories of all the failed pregnancy attempts of the past year began to haunt her.

Danyella and John had desired a baby from the moment they married. Starting a family felt like it should have come easily in their first two years as husband and wife. It had never occurred to them that the time line of their baby might be gripped in the hands of Father Time.

Their first detour came in the form of her breast cancer diagnosis promptly after their wedding. She hadn't been as emotional about the diagnosis as most twenty-seven-year-olds would have been. She didn't mind losing her breasts. She didn't even mind the year of back-to-back surgeries that followed. The only thing that crushed Danyella was knowing that someday she wouldn't get the opportunity to breastfeed her future children. After every appointment, every surgery, and every time she sat in recovery, she counted down the days till she could start her real life—one that included her unborn children.

The entire year following, Danyella and John embarked on the path of trying for a baby. On the third week of each month, Danyella crossed her fingers, held her breath, and followed the steps on the box of a new pregnancy test. She knew she was supposed to wait till the first day of her missed period, but patience wasn't her strongest virtue.

They had tried many times, too many to count. But that night, the thought of a positive test relieving her bad mood seemed to lift her spirits. *I already feel awful, so if it says no, I guess I'm not any worse off . . .* She smiled and unwrapped the box. She performed the memorized steps and placed the stick of opportunity as she called it on the counter. She knew that waiting for the results would prompt fear and worry. *A walk will do my busy mind some good.*

As she walked in the crisp winter air, she looked up at the towering fir trees that lined her neighborhood. Having grown up in the Pacific Northwest, she often took the lush, green landscape for granted, but that night, the trees reminded her of the stories that her aunt Samantha told her when she was a child—tales that gave those towering fir trees souls and mystical spirits that granted wishes to humans with pure hearts and peaceful intentions. She looked at them wishing they would grant her wish of her own children. She thought about how she had been dreaming of her future kids her whole life. She wasn't sure if all women desired to be mothers as much as she did, but she knew that there was no thought she loved more than that of being a mommy. Her favorite toys had always been baby dolls. Her favorite pastime had been playing house. She had always played the mother and treated her dolls with such care that her attention to them extended way beyond playtime. Eventually, her motherhood fantasy outlasted the typical years of such childish games, and she was forced to unwillingly move on to more age-appropriate things.

"What do you want to be when you grow up? And why?" Mrs. Elm, Danyella's first-grade teacher, had written across the whiteboard while instructing the children to answer the question in their notebooks.

Danyella looked around at her first-grade peers sitting in thought. Beaming, she tossed her feet back and forth under her chair as she proudly finished her assignment way before anyone else did.

Mrs. Elm walked the aisles making comments to each child about the tough decisions he or she was to make. Surprised to see Danyella's pencil at the side of a finished page, Mrs. Elm asked, "What did you decide you want to be when you grow up?"

Danyella proudly boasted, "I want to be a mommy!"

Mrs. Elm's face turned sour. "I don't think you understand the question, my dear," she said sternly.

"No! I do understand. I want to be a mommy!" Danyella replied with even more excitement.

10

Danyella recalled how Mrs. Elm had forcefully made her change what she had written that day from "mommy" to "daycare manager." But Mrs. Elm wasn't able to change Danyella's heart; she felt that everything was just in waiting till she would become a mother someday.

Marveling at the beauty of the winter sunset turning the sky a golden caramel, Danyella felt a powerful stroke of positivity. Despite her desire to feel sorry for herself, she couldn't ignore the feeling that urged her to smile. *You should be upset and crying right now because you just lost your supervisor position* her ego told her, but she felt deep inside that everything was working out the way it was supposed to. It was strange for her to have such intense opposing emotions at the same time. She suddenly remembered the pregnancy test at home. She anxiously picked up her pace.

She fumbled for her keys as she walked up the sidewalk to the string of apartment buildings. She followed the steps to her second-story apartment that overlooked the pool in the courtyard. She went in, made her way through the dark living room, and headed straight down the hallway to the bathroom. She visualized the outcome she desired. If she had learned anything about the law of attraction, it was that she needed to focus on what she desired while truly believing it already was hers. She closed her eyes and imagined the sight of the test reading positive. Next, she imagined telling John the good news, her belly growing large, and finally snuggling a beautiful baby in her arms. She felt a rush of happiness flood her heart and prompt a smile on her face. It felt like an endless stream of joy.

She knew she was ready to face reality. She opened the bathroom door and walked confidently up to the counter. Her eyes focused on two pink lines emanating from the pregnancy test. Her heart seemed to skip a beat as she realized the two lines read positive. She cupped her mouth with her hands. Sweet tears poured out of her happy eyes.

She looked at the beautiful scene that was unfolding in the mirror. She smiled at the reflection of her overjoyed self. One of the happiest moments was occurring, and she reminded herself to take it all in. *I'm pregnant!* She scoffed at the irony of one of her worst days ending with one of the best moments of her entire life. Her mind flooded with what to do next. *How will I surprise John?* She knew she was bad at keeping normal-sized secrets from him, and this was the biggest secret she had ever been responsible for holding. *I have to tell him tonight!*

When John arrived home from work, Danyella was impatiently waiting by the door. To prevent him from asking questions, she quickly distracted him with conversation. "I'm starving, honey, and I haven't cooked. Let's go out tonight. Hurry! Let's leave before you get hungry too," she said, sounding very convincing.

"Where are we going?" John asked while buckling his belt in the passenger seat.

Danyella dared not look at him; she was sure that if his dark-brown eyes met hers, he would surely figure it out. "How about our favorite place?" Danyella said in a tone that was unusually high-pitched.

"How sweet!" John replied with a playful smirk.

Arriving at the small Asian restaurant, they both looked at the booth where they had sat on their first date many years earlier. They smiled at one another, knowing exactly what the other was thinking.

"Just the two of you?" the waiter asked.

Danyella thought about saying, *Actually, three!* but she knew it wasn't the perfect moment to reveal her surprise. The elderly Asian waiter sluggishly picked up heir menus and forced a smile while ushering the happy couple to their seats. To Danyella's surprise, the waiter stopped at their memorable booth, flopped the menus on the table, and winked at Danyella, signaling that he remembered as well.

"Isn't this perfect?" Danyella asked with a tone of childish excitement.

"You're easily amused," John said while scanning his menu.

The waiter returned with water and hot tea. Danyella and John knew what they wanted; the waiter nodded at their requests that seemed to be so predictable that he didn't bother writing them down.

"Let's make a toast," she said while holding up her cup of warm tea.

"What should we toast to?" John asked with an intrigued smile. He matched her teacup, holding his in the air.

Danyella took a deep breath. "Cheers to us being pregnant!"

John's eyes shifted to her stomach. "Really, honey?"

"Yes!" Danyella replied happily.

"I'm going to be a dad?" John gasped. "How far along are you?"

"Well, I just found out, so probably a few weeks."

"This baby is so lucky to have you as its mom, honey!"

Danyella blushed at the thought of her baby being the lucky one. She felt as if she was the luckiest one.

The rest of the evening, they held hands and talked about their future, which would soon be filled with the joy of a new life instead of a new job opportunity. Danyella had never felt so happy.

That night, her excitement barely allowed her to sleep. And before her alarm had a chance to chime in the early morning hours, she jumped out of bed. "Good morning, little baby in there!" she said while rubbing her tummy. "Let's get ready for work!"

She wanted to wear something extra pretty to match her beautiful mood. She tossed several outfits on her bed before deciding on a pale-pink top with her tan work slacks. Pink felt fitting for some reason. Danyella didn't know why, but she felt confident about the clothes she had picked out. She brushed off the sign of intuition and focused on the positive feeling that everything was now perfect because she was pregnant.

When she got to work, her coworkers were buzzing with the news about the recent retraction of her supervisor position. Danyella just smiled and offered "Good morning!" to anyone who was bold enough to make eye contact with her.

"*Danyeeellllaaa!*" she heard as she neared her desk. It was her best friend, Kiki, peering over the cubicle wall that separated their desks. Kiki's wild auburn curls and piercing blue eyes matched her demanding expression of anticipation. "What happened yesterday afternoon? I saw you and Shawn enter the conference room, and after that, it was like you disappeared. At the end of the day, I received an email that said you had stepped down from the supervisor position. What happened? Spill it! I know you didn't step down!"

"Everything happens for a reason, Kiki. I didn't step down, but I'm no longer going to fill the position. I feel that fate stepped in and shined a light for me to go in a different direction," Danyella said calmly.

Kiki scrunched her face up. "Wow! You're taking this very well! Are you sure you're even human?" Kiki asked and winked at Danyella.

Danyella playfully rolled her eyes. Turning toward the corner of her cubicle to hang her coat, she caught the sight of Shawn sneaking into his office. He kept his eyes focused on the ground and quickly closed his office door. *He must feel so awkward,* Danyella thought. She decided to politely give him a few minutes before going to his office for their unavoidable talk. She gave a soft knock on his door and heard a nervous, "Come in."

She took a deep breath, slowly turned the handle, and pushed open the office door.

"Good morning," he announced with his back turned to her as he shuffled a stack of papers.

"May I?" she asked and waited for his attention. She gestured at the door.

"Of course!" he added quickly as his face flushed pink.

They sat in a few seconds of awkward air before Danyella broke the silence. "I feel I deserve the real explanation for what happened."

"This is completely one hundred percent my fault. When I asked you to apply for the position, I was under the impression that your experience satisfied the requirements. I pushed your application through to the top because you were my first pick. It wasn't until I announced you as the hired applicant that the hiring department said anything. The moment I got that phone call, it felt like someone had kicked me in the stomach. I'm sorry, Danyella." His face turned from nervous to relieved as he expelled his explanation.

Danyella paused. She knew there were bigger forces at play than just the hiring department coming down hard on a manager's decision.

"Thank you for telling me the truth. It is what it is. I believe there are no accidents because everything happens for a reason, so stop blaming yourself. It'll all work out exactly how it's supposed to," she said in a gentle tone. She felt Shawn's shock as she delivered her unexpected response.

"You know, I told them the minute you left the meeting yesterday that the way you handled things was why I hired you in the first place. No one else would handle this situation the way you have, Danyella."

She tried not to blush as she accepted the compliment with a nod and a gentle smile. "Have a good day, Shawn," she said, walking out of his office.

Walking back to her desk, she felt the eyes of several coworkers scan her face to see if they could obtain any sign about the private meeting. She knew the place was buzzing with what the real story was, but no one had the courage to ask. She smiled all the way to her desk. There was only one thing on her mind: *I'm going to be a stay-at-home mommy!*

CHAPTER 2

9:22

Telling her loved ones about her baby on the way was half the fun for Danyella. She tried to think of creative ways, but sometimes the urge to just blurt it out was too strong. She was looking forward to telling Kiki her little secret at lunch, but as she sat at her desk anxiously trying to work, her impatience intensified. She stared at her computer screen trying to motivate herself to get to work. Her stomach felt a turn of excitement every time she thought about her baby growing in her. It was hard to focus. Danyella decided she couldn't wait another minute and began searching for the best way to tell Kiki.

The two had been good friends for several years. They had met at work and instantly felt the calling of a deep friendship. Danyella felt that she had known Kiki for several lifetimes on the first day they met. Kiki felt the same way about Danyella, and they often spent a good part of their workdays laughing and sharing stories. Kiki had been there for Danyella through her breast cancer recovery and the last year of trying to get pregnant. Kiki had held Danyella's hand and cried right along with her each time Danyella received her dreaded period each month. She was positive that Kiki would be just as thrilled as she was to receive the good news about the baby on its way. She grabbed a pencil and a yellow sticky note. She wrote a message, folded it up, and handed it to Kiki.

Kiki was lost in her work but smiled with curiosity as Danyella handed her what seemed to be a secretive note over the cubicle wall. Kiki unfolded the note and read, "I am pregnant." Kiki squealed with delight while getting lost in the moment and forgetting where they were.

"Really?" Kiki asked.

"Yes!" a beaming Danyella whispered.

"Oh my gosh! *Awww*, that makes me wanna cry!"

"Don't cry! You'll make me cry!" Danyella said, chuckling.

"This is why you're beaming on a day you should be bummed. I knew you were taking this job thing way too well, Danyella."

"Everything does happen for a reason. I guess my baby just knew I was going to need to stay home soon."

The women embraced and felt one of the best joys of all time, the excitement of new life. After their momentary celebration, they scurried back to their desks.

Danyella looked at her clock: 9:22. She had to get to work, but the numbers made her pause. That was the third time she had glanced at the clock at exactly twenty-two minutes after the hour. She brushed off what seemed to be a coincidence and started catching up on neglected emails; several of them were from coworkers, asking why she had stepped down from the supervisor position. She scanned past the unimportant emails, searching for job-related ones. Her computer flashed a notification on her screen as another annoying gossip email floated into her inbox. Her eyes moved straight to the boldfaced number of unread messages—22. *There's that number again. What do I need to know about this number, angels?* She did not believe in coincidences; she believed that spiritually, everything had a purpose. She felt that the number of times she was seeing that number was significant. She saw 22 a dozen more times, along with 922, a handful of times that day.

When she arrived home, she barely noticed John waiting eagerly at the door to help his pregnant wife take off her coat. "How was your day, honey?"

"Good," Danyella said distractedly. "I think I need to call my sister."

"Why? Is everything all right?"

"I've seen numbers really close to her birthday, and it wasn't just a couple of times … It's every hour or more. And the only thing that makes sense is that maybe I'm supposed to talk to her. Maybe the angels are trying to have me help her. I know it sounds funny, but why else would these numbers keep showing up like that?"

"So you saw her birthday numbers? Where?"

"It's not her birthday that I keep seeing. It's the day before her birthday. But I keep seeing that date and the number twenty-two everywhere. I mean, I've seen it way too many times today to say it was by chance."

John was smiling at his wife adoringly as she grabbed her phone and called her sister. He watched her dramatically wave her hands in the air as if her sister could see her. Danyella turned around to find him playfully laughing at her, but she didn't mind; she knew that he found her spiritual connections endearing. She playfully rolled her eyes in response to his gawking at her.

"Well, now I'm really baffled," Danyella said as she hung up. "Jacky says she's fine, and she can't think of why she would need me to talk with her." Danyella scrunched up her face in confusion.

"Maybe you're just accidentally seeing the same numbers for no reason," John said, grinning and raising his eyebrows.

"Since there are no such things as coincidences, I'll have to say you're wrong," she said playfully while leaning in for a kiss.

The next morning, Danyella woke before her alarm. She knew she had woken up early because John was still lying next to her on the other side of the bed. She rolled over to check the time. She froze when she saw the illuminated numbers on the clock: 3:22 a.m. *There's that twenty-two again.* She felt a warm fuzziness all over her body; it felt nice like the feeling she experienced when hugging John. *I'm not sure what this number is all about, but I know it must be important.* She closed her eyes and tried to fall back asleep.

The following morning at work, Danyella pondered the numbers she had seen so repetitively. *If it's not Jacky's birthday, and nine twenty-two doesn't ring any bells for me, what could it signify?* Suddenly, her phone chimed, notifying her that she had received a text. It was from her cousin Abigail, congratulating her on her pregnancy and asking, "When's the due date?"

"Don't know. I've been too excited to figure that out," Danyella texted.

"Look it up!" Abigail texted back without hesitation.

Danyella searched the internet for a website that would calculate her due date. *Being pregnant is fun!* She plugged in the numbers, hit enter, and held her breath. She choked a little as she read the due date: 9/22. The joyful moment felt as if time stoped and lasted several hours. She wanted to scream with joy, but she remained composed. *This whole time, it was my baby communicating with me! She's on her way!* "Wait ... Did I just say her?" she questioned herself out loud.

Kiki heard Danyella's self-directed question over the cubicle wall. "Did you just say what?"

"Kiki, I have lots to tell you at lunch."

Kiki was the only friend who would understand what Danyella was about to share. Kiki seemed to have spiritual views similar to hers, and she enjoyed hearing new abstract ways of looking at things. But then a bit of doubt set in. *What if Kiki thinks I'm making all this up, like John?* She worried about Kiki not taking her seriously, but she remembered just how many times she had seen the number 922 repeatedly in the last twenty-four hours, which helped her regain her confidence that this was her baby's way of communicating.

At lunch, Kiki giggled while Danyella shared her beautiful adventure.

"Oh, I'm so happy for you! Motherhood is so beautiful! And your relationship with this baby is so strong and breathtaking. If I could have a hundred more babies, I would!" Kiki said in a dreamy state watching her friend glow with happiness.

"This baby is just so amazing, and it's only the beginning! I can't imagine when I finally get to meet her!" Danyella gasped at the thought.

"I can't wait to meet her too!"

The two friends smiled at each other, and Danyella felt safer knowing she had someone to confide in about the most powerful relationship of her life.

Morning sickness ensued like normal, and Danyella watched as her body began to slowly change. By the time she was ten weeks along, she had shared the good news with family and friends while ignoring the standard twelve-week sharing rule that most people recommended. Her grandparents cried, her sister screamed, and her friends jumped up and down with delight.

Danyella made sure to give one person the news carefully—her cousin Christy, who had been trying for a baby too. The two had always been very close, and life seemed to happen in similar timelines for them; they had graduated from college together, they had married within a year of each other, and they had started trying for their firstborns at the same time. Danyella took a deep breath as she looked at her beautiful cousin and worked up the courage to deliver the good news. She was nervous, but she knew Christy would view Danyella's success as her own.

"So I've been thinking about this trying-for-a-baby thing," Danyella said as they were driving to lunch.

"Yeah, it's been tough for us for sure. What about you and John?"

"Well ..." Danyella hesitated. "John and I recently stopped trying."

"Oh my gosh! I totally understand. It's a lot of pressure. More than I ever thought. I mean, our parents and family mean well, but they ask all the time if I'm pregnant yet, and every time, I want to yell, 'We're trying, OK!'" Christy laughed trying to lighten the emotion of the conversation. Danyella giggled; she knew how Christy felt.

"So what's your plan?"

"Well, we aren't trying any longer because we don't need to try anymore," Danyella said while trying to catch Christy's glimpse.

"Oh my gosh! Are you pregnant?"

"Yes!" Danyella squealed.

Christy screamed with happiness. "You have no idea how excited I am for you!"

"Well, I do, because I can imagine how I'd feel for you if you were pregnant. And I'm sure I will soon, Christy."

With hugs and happy tears, they were full of love and appreciation for one another and for the new life they were going to soon meet. They spent the afternoon talking all things baby.

Danyella's and John's families were thrilled at the news; it was just what their families needed—someone new and exciting to make life less dull. Danyella's mother was almost as excited as Danyella and John.

Danyella's mom beamed as she handed Danyella a plain paper gift bag with tissue on top. They smiled endearingly at one another, and Danyella rushed to open the surprise. Her hands felt the soft cotton fabric as she pulled out a one-piece, button-up pajama outfit with little yellow baby ducks printed all around. And as if the fabric weren't darling enough, there were two little yellow duck bills at the feet. Danyella didn't have words to express how precious she thought it was. She hugged her mom and snuggled the empty baby pajamas next to her face to display how much the little gesture meant to her. "It's perfect, Mom! Thank you."

"You're welcome, honey. I know it's a little early, but I just couldn't wait when I saw this outfit," she said with a bashful smile.

"Can you just imagine a little baby body in this?" Danyella was beaming.

"I can! That's why I couldn't resist buying it! Hurry up and grow, little baby, so we can put you in these pj's," Danyella's mom said in an endearing voice as she rubbed her daughter's belly.

Once at home, Danyella delightfully hung the tiny yellow duckling pajamas in the front of her closet. It was a sweet reminder every time she opened the closet door. It made the pregnancy thing seem so much more real, and it prompted sweet daydreams about the baby that would someday fill those little footies.

CHAPTER 3

A CHANGE IN DIRECTION

Twelve weeks went by in a blink of an eye, and Danyella started to feel the sleepiness side effect of her pregnancy. Her weekends were filled with long naps and hunting for her favorite meals. After a long, cozy, Saturday snooze on the couch, Danyella woke to find John watching her sleep.

"You look so peaceful while you sleep," he said softly. Danyella blushed and waved him off playfully as if she didn't believe him. "Let's get going to Uncle Bernie's surprise party, Sleeping Beauty," John said with a gentle smirk.

Danyella loved the way he always had a spark of romance in his eyes when he looked at her; that made her feel special. "OK. I'll freshen up, and we can go."

On the way to the party, Danyella received a phone call from her dad. "How's my little girl and my little grandbaby doing?" he asked with more excitement in his voice than she had ever remembered hearing before. She loved hearing him so excited, and she loved hearing the word *grandbaby.*

"We're doing great, Dad! I took another long power nap, and we're on our way to visit John's family for Uncle Bernie's birthday."

"Oh, OK. That sounds like fun. I won't keep you then. Just wanted to remind you how much I love you."

"Love you too, Dad. Thanks for checking up on us."

Danyella smiled at how thoughtful her dad had been. Being pregnant changed Danyella's and John's role in their families; it was like they had graduated from a kindergarten-type level marriage and were moving on to a big-league marriage. Both families delighted in rubbing Danyella's belly and patting John on the back. Danyella embraced her new role. It felt nice, as if something before had always been missing, and now it had finally arrived.

During dinner, Danyella's phone rang. She excused herself and left the bustling room. It was her mother; a good feeling came over her, as always, when she heard from her mom. "Hi, Mom!"

"Hi, honey. How are you and that baby doing today?"

"We're great. I've been really sleepy all day long. I took a long nap before going to John's uncle's party, but I'm sure that's just part of pregnancy." Danyella was gushing with delight.

"Yes, I remember being very tired when I was pregnant with you too. It's normal. I was just calling because I kept thinking about you today. I couldn't get you off my mind, so I thought I'd call."

"That's sweet. You and Dad both." Danyella chuckled.

"Maybe we're just thrilled at the thought of being grandparents!" Danyella's mother laughed.

"I love your calls either way, Mom."

"Love you too, honey! I'll let you get back to the party."

Danyella's heart was full as she got off the phone. *Both parents calling in the same hour? How strange!* Danyella thought.

Her parents had been divorced since Danyella was a baby. They were kind, loving people, but they drove each other crazy. Danyella couldn't remember a day when her parents were together. Jacky and Danyella had grown up splitting their time with each parent. Danyella had been happier traveling back and forth between the two homes than she thought she would have been living with parents who were miserable together. She had witnessed her parents' distaste for one another on several occasions, which reminded Danyella why they were no longer together.

Her parents calling in the same hour felt like an unfamiliar comfort, almost as if they had something in common; that had seemed almost impossible to Danyella while growing up. She was in a sort of heavenly bliss receiving love from both parents in the same afternoon.

That night after the party, Danyella felt restless. She was tossing and turning in bed. The clock seemed to taunt her as she stared at the ceiling. She felt as if she were waiting for something to happen. But her eyes grew heavy, and she finally drifted off to sleep.

Several minutes later, she was jolted awake by a sharp pain in her abdomen. Her sleepy mind grasped for answers. The pain felt like sharp, harsh menstrual cramps. *Oh no, my baby! Everything's all right ... Everything's all right ...* She tried to lie to reassure herself.

Just as she was calming down, she felt something damp between her legs. She jumped out of bed and ran to the bathroom to examine her body. She sat on the toilet and saw that her underwear was filled with blood. Her heart sank. *This can't be happening!* But it was happening. No matter how much she tried to talk herself out of the reality of what was going on, she knew it was over. She started bleeding profusely. She called frantically for John, who was asleep in the other room.

John scrambled to his feet after being awakened by her panicked scream of his name. John's face was struck with terror when he got to the bathroom and saw her hunched over in pain on the toilet.

"Honey! Oh my gosh! We need to go to the emergency room!" John yelled in terror.

"The baby's gone, honey," Danyella sobbed.

"What do you mean? How?"

"I'm having a miscarriage," Danyella could barely finish her sentence before curling into another string of pain. It was a type of emotional and physical pain Danyella had never felt before, and the emotional pain overshadowed the extreme physical pain.

John ran to his phone and called the midwife's office. Through her sobs, Danyella heard John relating the details. His sorrowful yeses and I understands were all Danyella needed to confirm the horrible reality. The pain and blood indicated that nothing could be done medically to save her baby. Although it was very painful, a miscarriage would not be harmful to endure at home. John quietly hung up while Danyella lay shaking in pain on the bathroom floor. Her tears felt like her only source of comfort as she shook with each wave of pain that followed.

Nothing in her life had prepared her for such a traumatic event. She felt stuck physically and emotionally. She couldn't bear to leave the bathroom that night despite John's gentle urging to return to their room. The cold tile floor seemed like a better match for her sorrow than a warm bed. There was no place for any kind of comfort in this depth of the despair. She didn't know how she would ever face the world again without her baby. Just like parts of her future slipping away from her grasp, her tears fell onto the floor as she hugged her empty belly and cried herself to sleep.

But when she woke, she was forced to face the world without her baby. She couldn't understand why the world just kept on going as if nothing had happened. *Don't the stars, the moon, the universe understand? My baby's gone! There is no fucking world without my baby!*

She couldn't think past the present. There was no future in her mind. There was nothing but her pain. She missed the presence of her child's spirit that she had always felt while pregnant. She couldn't find her anymore. She knew her baby's spirit had passed to the other side. Danyella felt alone. She felt a separation inside that she had never experienced before. She felt as if suddenly nothing mattered. Nothing felt right, and her mind urged her to believe that nothing ever would. She was lost in what felt like an eternity of pain. She wanted to sleep and never wake up. She finally hobbled to her bed and collapsed into the sheets. She pulled the covers over her puffy face and did the only thing that made sense. She went to sleep.

When she couldn't sleep any longer, she just lay there staring at the wall, trying to find the missing feeling of her baby's spirit. No matter how hard she focused, she felt only the absence of the energy that had once surrounded her. She felt that every good feeling had been ripped away.

In the early evening, John convinced Danyella to take a shower and sit up in bed. The zombie-eyed look on Danyella's face worried him. He did his best to do as she wished, but he felt as if he were aiding her slow demise. She was expressionless; he saw no life in her eyes. It was as if she had died along with their baby. He clung to his faith that this was normal for a mother who had lost her child. He hoped her depression would pass any day, perhaps any hour. *I just need to give her time.*

John couldn't completely understand what Danyella was experiencing. He felt sad for the loss of their child, but he saw that for Danyella, it was much more than losing the hope for a child. It seemed to him that Danyella had lost a part of herself. That evening, he ignored her request for no visitors and called her mom.

"She's taking this really hard," John explained quietly over the phone. "She said she doesn't want to see anyone, but I think she needs her mom and her sister." He cleared his throat. "I don't know how to help her through this the way she needs." He wanted to cry at the thought of not being enough for his wife during one of the biggest hurdles they had ever faced.

"Of course, honey. Jacky and I'll be right over. Thanks for calling," she said lovingly.

John sighed in relief after the call and began preparing dinner though he knew Danyella wouldn't eat it. His mind drifted to his memory of their first date. He had been anxious as they sat across from one another nervously scanning the menu and glancing up often, each looking into the other's eyes. He didn't want to take his eyes off her. He couldn't concentrate when her deep-blue eyes met his; that made him ask silly questions. He had asked if she wanted children someday.

Her face lit up with passion he had never seen in any woman before, and she said, "Yes I do! I've dreamed of having children for most of my life. When I marry, I'll want to have children, and when I do, I'll be a stay-at-home mom."

Having children wasn't a topic he normally brought up until the fifth or sixth date, but with Danyella, the conversation felt oddly fitting. He remembered the twinkle he'd seen in her eyes.

Eight years later, he was desperate to see that same glow in her face that she reserved for their future children. A sharp knock on the door broke his pleasant daydreams and snapped him back to reality. He sighed in relief when he saw his mother-in-law through the glass peep-hole of the front door.

Time has no measure on an occasion like death. Danyella felt as if she had been lying in bed and staring at the ceiling for days. She did everything her sad mind could muster up to repel the constant thought that rang, *She's gone. She's gone. My baby's gone ... What did I do wrong? Maybe it was the tea I drank before I found out I was pregnant? Or maybe that sushi I ate before I knew I wasn't supposed to? How could I have been so stupid! How can I go on without my child?*

The sight of her mom and her sister walking into the bedroom brought her back from her thoughts and reminded her that it was real. She was alive, and this was all actually happening. She sobbed uncontrollably as she flopped into her mom's embrace. The three women cried and mourned the loss of what might have been. Little did anyone know that Danyella was crying for the loss of so much more.

CHAPTER 4

LIFE AFTER DEATH

The next few weeks were numbing for Danyella. She didn't try to make sense of it all. In fact, she didn't try to think about it much. On the sixth day of her bereavement leave from work, Jacky called her. Danyella knew something was wrong the moment she picked up the phone.

"Hello?" Danyella answered sluggishly.

"Danyella ..." Jacky said in a quaky voice.

"Hi, Jacky. What's wrong?"

"It's Grandma. She ... *Ummm* ... She isn't doing so well. Things just took a turn for the worse this week, and we're all saying our goodbyes."

Danyella took a deep breath. She had known for a while that this day was coming, but she had never expected it to happen when she was emotionless.

"What did the doctor say?"

"He said that at this point, her mind is gone and that we need to make her as comfortable as possible for her last few days. I'm flying out tonight to be with her. I'm not sure if I'll even make it in time, according to Aunt Melissa, but I'm going to try."

"Give her hugs and kisses for me, OK?" Danyella asked holding back the knot welling in her throat.

"I will. We know you're going through a lot right now and don't expect you to make a sudden trip. She probably won't even remember who I am, but I want to be there."

"Thank you, sis," Danyella managed to get out before saying goodbye and quickly hanging up the phone to break down and cry. As the tears ran down her face, she remembered a phrase her grandma always used to say: "When death comes knocking, it always comes in pairs." She had never understood that phrase as a child. She wasn't ever sure what her grandma meant by it. But sitting there with the heartache of two losses, she felt that her grandma's words were meant for that very moment.

Danyella's grandma had always been fun, adventurous, and extremely sassy. But even when her grandma was directing her sassiness at Danyella, she always had a good point to whatever she was being so opinionated about. She could put anyone in his or her place, but her stunning good looks always helped soften that blow.

What she loved most about her grandma was how when she was in a room, everyone knew it. She had a certain charisma about her that just brought everyone around her to life. She had the gift of gab, and maybe that was where Danyella had gotten hers. She sat in tears thinking of all their late-night talks when her grandma would come visit. Her grandma had always slept in Danyella's room. The two acted more like girlfriends staying up late and chatting about boys and gossiping than granddaughter and a grandmother. She would miss that about her grandma, but she knew that death didn't mean life was over; it just meant that she wouldn't be around physically for Danyella to see. She would just have to get used to finding her grandma in new ways. Danyella felt the loss of her grandma even before she was gone, which helped her grieve quickly.

Danyella wished that she could feel some gratitude for the loss of her baby the way she did for the departure of her grandma. Maybe it was the expected death after a long and happy life that she could wrap her mind around more easily than losing a life before ever getting to hold her sweet baby. She wasn't positive about why she couldn't feel content about the loss of her baby; she just knew she felt empty.

Death before birth was really a strange concept for Danyella. To her, this baby was as real as anyone could get, but to the world, it was just a fetus that hadn't made it. She struggled with how others tried to comfort her and her husband by saying odd, insensitive things: "It's OK. Just make another one" or "That's why I never told anyone until my fourth month." Danyella didn't understand how people could be so coldhearted, but she did her best to tune them out and not let their ignorant comments get her down. She began to numb herself emotionally from the people around her just to make it through each day.

During her bereavement leave, she hadn't gotten out of her pajamas, but her sorrow couldn't last forever. The world kept turning even though she thought it should stop and cry along with her. It didn't. She finally got to a place where she knew she had to go forward and face the world. She needed to get back to her routine and feel normal again if normal was what life after the death of a child could ever be.

When her alarm clock went off Monday morning, Danyella rolled her eyes. Getting out of bed was harder than she had imagined. She pulled herself out of bed, made her way to the bathroom, and turned on the shower. Standing in front of the bathroom mirror, she wiped her blond hair out of her hazy blue eyes and stared at the lifeless reflection staring back at her. The dark circles under her eyes seemed to match her deathly mood. "I can do this," she said in a somewhat convincing tone. Danyella rubbed her face vigorously with both hands before undressing and entering the warm stream of water.

Moment by moment, she felt better. Getting herself ready did seem to help. *What to wear?* she wondered. *All black?* she asked herself sarcastically. Opening her closet, she saw the little ducky footy pajamas. The sight hit her like a ghost standing stalemate in her path. Her breath quivered. Her eyes filled with stinging tears. She snatched up the pj's, stumbled backward, and slid down the wall as her tears began to flow. She wanted to scream. Yell. Run. But instead, she sank to her knees and cried into the little lifeless outfit.

This pain was the worst heartbreak she had ever felt. Nothing had ever shaken her quite as much as this. Now, she wasn't so sure she was ready to face the world or an office full of people for that matter. But she was sick of spending so much time running away from her aching thoughts, so she grudgingly put on her makeup, straightened her hair, got dressed, and went back to work.

At work, she tried to focus on her job so others wouldn't have time to talk to talk with her about what she was going through. But Kiki was another story. As soon as Danyella caught sight of her best friend, she felt some relief. *Someone who'll be realistic and understand what I'm going through.*

Kiki didn't even stop at her own desk to drop off her coat and purse; she headed straight to Danyella. Neither said a word. They just embraced and allowed their tears to fall. Danyella wasn't aware of it, but Kiki had been through a miscarriage with her first pregnancy several years before they had met. The pain of Danyella's broken heart brought back the heartache of Kiki's past.

"I'm not going to ask you any stupid questions like how you're doing because I know there's no good that can come from that. But I'm here if you need to talk it out or if you want me to talk. Whatever you need, I'll be here with you, OK?"

Danyella knew it was just like Kiki to be there right when she needed her. "I'm just lost right now, you know? I miss my baby, and it feels so surreal, like it's here and happening but I can't believe it. It doesn't feel right." Danyella said while sniffing back tears.

"The only thing that can heal this type of pain is time, sweetheart." Kiki caressed Danyella's shoulder. "People are going to say some really stupid and ignorant things about this, but don't take it personally. They don't mean it. They're uncomfortable and don't really know how to comfort you, so they'll be awkward, OK?"

Danyella nodded and forced a smile for her loving friend.

She worked that day with an invisible sign on her forehead that read, Please Don't Talk to Me! She kept her eyes glued to her computer screen and keyboard, avoiding making eye contact with anyone. She snuck out of the office with Kiki for an early lunch and ducked into her cubicle before the others returned. Danyella was normally a very social person who greeted everyone with a friendly hello, so with the sudden shift to her normal behavior, the office was buzzing with gossip about why she had been absent.

"I heard her grandma died."

36

"No, I heard she lost her baby."

"I'm not so sure it's her grandma, because don't you think people expect old people to die? She seems way too sad for that." Thus went conversations around the water cooler.

Kiki had finally confessed to a few close coworkers, and they spread the word. By that afternoon, everyone in the office knew about Danyella's miscarriage. And just as Kiki had warned Danyelle, people said stupid and hurtful things.

"I'm sorry to hear about your pregnancy," one young coworker said with a disgustingly sad look on her face.

"Thank you," Danyella said softly.

"Was this your first pregnancy?"

"It was my first baby, yes." Danyella said emphasizing the word *baby*.

"I hear it's really common. It happens to most women," the young girl said, trying to sound comforting.

Danyella just looked at the woman's pale face and held back her tears while grasping onto Kiki's words, *Forgive them.* Danyella didn't care how common miscarriages were. She didn't care if most women experienced such a loss. No one but she had ever suffered the loss of her baby. *And no one in the world is* my *baby!*

The rest of the I'm sorrys blurred together as coworker after coworker got up the courage to extend their awkward sympathies to her. By the end of the day, she was out of tissues. Her return to the world without her baby had challenged her in a way she had never expected; it required her to love everyone around her unconditionally. With Kiki's advice so present in her mind, she began to thank the universe for everyone who had tried to console her, even if it felt as if they had reopened a painful wound with their insensitive comments.

Pretty soon, Danyella's days and nights became easier. Eventually, she started to feel like herself again. She praised herself several weeks later when she could finally get through a day without crying. Her baby remained on her mind, but day by day, she found it easier to live life, even if it was without her baby.

One chilly spring evening, Danyella hadn't noticed it, but she was back to her blissful self. As she cleaned up after dinner, she found herself mentally going over all the wonderful things she had experienced that day. She had been thankful, earlier that day, for her delicious breakfast sandwich and warm tea as she had watched the sun rise from her office window. She had been thankful for the joy and laughter she had shared with Kiki that afternoon on their walk. She had been thankful for the amazing dinner John had surprised her with as she walked through the door that evening. *What a wonderful life I have*, she said to herself, smiling from ear to ear.

Because she was focused on her wonderful feeling of gratitude, she almost didn't notice the bright pink light that was filling her apartment and creeping its way around the corner into the kitchen, to join her where she stood at the sink. She scrunched up her face in confusion. The pink light was so beautiful that it almost distracted her from the oddness of its placement. *Where's that light coming from?* She went to the living room to find the light's source and gasped at the most breathtaking sunset she had ever seen, lighting up the sky in an array of pinks and purples.

She grabbed her phone and ran out on the porch. Her eyes widened at the fuchsia sky. She took several photos. None of them completely captured the beauty that her heart could feel and her eyes could see. To her, the sunset was more than a sunset; it was a magical sight. She knew, with all her heart, that it was her daughter. It was the first time she had felt her daughter since that dreadful night on the bathroom floor. This sign felt like being able to hold a loved one she missed terribly. Tears of happiness trickled down her cheeks as she smiled toward the sky. "I miss you, baby girl!" she whispered. She knew in that moment that she didn't care how she was getting to see or feel her daughter's presence; she was just thankful that she was getting a chance to find her in this new way.

Day by day, she began to sense her daughter by her side once again. She started seeing the number twenty-two everywhere, just like before. It showed up as totals on things she was thinking about buying and dates her family and friends picked for special events. It would be twenty-two minutes after the hour almost every time she glanced at a clock. It was like having her favorite person with her at all times. Her daughter was very good at reminding her that she was near. Danyella felt renewed by her baby's presence even if it was just in spirit.

CHAPTER 5

AIN'T NO MOUNTAIN HIGH ENOUGH

One sunny Saturday morning, while John was playing golf with his friends, Danyella stared out the window as she sipped her morning tea and wondered what this lovely day was going to bring her. *It's so pretty outside, too pretty to waste the day sitting in the house.*

First, she called Kiki and groaned when she reached her voicemail. Jacky was out of town on a business trip, and everyone else seemed to have plans. "I guess it's just you and me, baby girl!" Danyella said dramatically as she thought about spending the day enjoying the company of someone who wasn't on earth.

"First to pedicures!" Danyella proclaimed as she grabbed her keys and headed to the car. She reminded herself that it might be best to start talking to her daughter in her mind once she left the house. She knew she would get weird looks from strangers if she started having a conversation with someone who wasn't there for others to see.

"Ain't no mountain high enough," the car radio blared when she turned the key in the ignition. Danyella felt her daughter's energetic nudge and knew that the song was from her. "Well aren't you cute, little girl!" She laughed and started to sing along. She felt excited to find her daughter in this new way. Danyella felt loved.

"Ain't no mountain high enough, ain't no valley low enough, and no river wide enough to keep me from getting to you, babe!" Marvin Gaye's old song played. Tears welled up in Danyella's eyes as she listened to the lyrics. She knew exactly what her daughter was saying to her, and she felt the same way. There was nothing that could keep them apart, not even death itself.

Danyella arrived at the nail salon wearing her biggest smile. She couldn't hide her excitement for the new love she was experiencing. The nail tech didn't acknowledge her bubbly mood; she ushered her in, as usual, and pointed to the shelves of nail polish so Danyella could pick out a color. Danyella felt overwhelmed by the thousands of choices. *Oh but they're all so pretty!* She suddenly felt inspired to let her daughter pick a color, maybe one with the number twenty-two, but there were only twenty shelves. *I'll have to get creative. Let's see … Eleven and eleven equals twenty-two.* She counted up eleven shelves and then counted over to the eleventh bottle … a sparkling pale pink. "Good pick!" she said out loud, forgetting about her recent rule. She blushed and looked around to see if anyone had caught her talking out loud, but no one had seemed to notice. She giggled as she blushed.

That summer, everyone, including her cousin Christy, was getting pregnant—everyone except her. Danyella was of course happy for her cousin, but it felt like something was missing. She tried to keep her focus on her happiness for others, but each time they revealed their joyful news, she felt lost. She would force a smile and hold back her tears and then politely excuse herself to cry alone. She wished so badly that she was experiencing all the new adventures they were finding themselves on. When they complained about pregnancy heartburn and how uncomfortable their bellies were, she was wishing she could be in their shoes.

Since the miscarriage, she had been worried about trying for another baby. The heartache and emotional pain of this loss already felt unbearable. Her fear of another miscarriage prevented John and her from trying again. But after six months, her desire for a baby was stronger than ever, so they began once again. Each month when Danyella got her period, she fell apart a little, but a few days after her periods, she would bounce back to being positive and determined. It was an emotional roller coaster that seemed to be stuck on repeat.

Danyella's patience had been wearing thin, but on this positive day, when she and Kiki were on their way to lunch at the hospital cafeteria, Danyella felt a surge of sureness that this could be the month she would become pregnant. "This could be it! This could be the month!" Danyella said with excitement.

Kiki smiled back. "I hope so!"

"Me too! I have a good feeling! Meet you at our usual table. I'm going to run to the restroom."

"I'll save your seat," Kiki replied.

Walking into the restroom, Danyella smiled at her confident reflection in the oversized mirror as she passed the long counter of sinks. As she sat down on the toilet, her eyes fell on a spot of bright-red blood on her beige underwear. Next, she checked the stream of urine that flowed in a shade of pink. She exhaled deeply as her heart sank and her throat knotted up. She felt like she couldn't breathe. And then, the tears came so rapidly that she pulled her knees to her chest and began to bawl. Again, she felt alone. She wanted to be positive, but the pain of the moment overshadowed her desire. She felt defeated. After her cry in the bathroom stall, she yearned for a change. *What I'm doing isn't working! And it sure doesn't feel good either!* The sting of her unwanted reality convinced her to do what she knew worked best—she would write out a thankful list.

As she walked up to the lunchroom table, her puffy eyes and distressed expression stunned Kiki. "Danyella, what happened?"

Danyella couldn't respond without folding into another stream of tears. "My period has arrived. I'm trying to be grateful, but this feels so hard." She cried while sliding into the chair across from Kiki.

"Oh honey! I am so sorry! This is one of the hardest things life has to offer," Kiki said with empathetic eyes. She extended her arm across the table to rub Danyella's hands in comfort.

"I'm going to head back to my desk instead of eating lunch today. I don't feel like eating anymore." Danyella wiped the tears from her eyes and rose from her seat.

Kiki didn't have to say a word; she just nodded.

Danyella averted her eyes from her friend and walked away. When she reached her cubicle, she quickly searched for a pen and a blank piece of paper. Sitting down, she felt sure about moving her energy in a different direction. She began to write.

I am thankful for my period because it means I have the ability to make a baby.

I am thankful for my husband's willingness to cocreate this life with me.

I am thankful that my body is young and healthy and able to create life.

I am thankful that this journey has strengthened my desire and brought it closer to my heart.

I am thankful for the patience this journey has built.

I am thankful for my relationship with my baby before my pregnancy.

I am thankful Kiki has been a shoulder for me to cry on.

I am thankful I have the knowledge that someday I will be pregnant because it's something I desire and my desires are always created.

I am thankful that my baby chose me.

I am thankful that I am pregnant.

Danyella always ended her thankful lists with her desires in the present tense. It felt good to read it out loud that way. She looked at her gratitude list and felt better. She felt ready to chase her dreams again. She circled number one at the top of her list. *I'll tell myself this every time I get my period. I'll be thankful for my periods because they're the reason I'm able to conceive a child.*

Danyella watched her pregnant friends' and relatives' bellies grow and grow. She stayed hopeful and optimistic as she fell more and more in love with the communication between her and her baby's spirit. It was a special kind of relationship that couldn't be explained, but it fulfilled her in so many ways. Her baby understood her immediately on every subject without any resistance. Danyella felt at home, knowing someone understood her at such a deep level.

Before she knew it, it was September 22. She woke with mixed emotions. She was ecstatic that her baby's day was finally here, but it felt odd because her baby wasn't … well, not in physical form, at least. She decided that it would be a blessed day, a day full of praise and joy in honor of her baby. She planned a special dinner for her and John—steak, red wine, roses, and candles, all on the deck.

John came home that evening with a bouquet of roses for her as well. Danyella and the baby had been on his mind all day. He was hoping to find her in good spirits. "How was your day, honey?" he asked tentatively.

"It was great! How was yours?"

"I thought a lot about our baby today of course. And every time I looked at the clock, it was twenty-two minutes after the hour!" John replied with a soft smile.

"*Awww*, honey! Our baby was saying hi to you!" Danyella said excited to have her not very spiritual husband sharing his spiritual experience.

"Yeah, I guess so," John replied.

They made their way to the deck and to the romantic table setting. He was relieved that she was celebrating the day instead of crying about it.

Sitting down, Danyella reached out her hands to begin a prayer. "Thank you for this amazing dinner with my husband in this beautiful fall weather. A special day to celebrate a special part of our lives. Instead of focusing on what we've lost, today, I want to celebrate what we have. Thank you, Love, for this journey. Amen." She squeezed his hand. "I made it just the way you like it!" She winked at him, and John smiled in amazement.

That night, the happy couple made love rather than trying for a baby as they had been doing for several weeks. Danyella wrapped herself up in her husband's touch and felt more connected to him physically than she had in a long time. In the midst of her husband's sweet kisses down her back, Danyella realized she hadn't once thought about trying to conceive. Ending in complete satisfaction, Danyella fell asleep quickly.

John gazed at his wife sleeping so peacefully. They had endured so much pain over the last year that seeing his wife back to her normal bliss was a gift. He loved Danyella, and in that moment, he felt his love deepen and expand beyond what he had believed was possible. He wasn't the praying type of man, but that night while lying next to his sleeping wife, he said a prayer: *Dear Lord ... or whoever you are, if you can hear me ... please help me give my wife a baby. She really deserves a child. I want to see her as a mother. It's her lifelong dream, and I know she'll be the best mother. This baby will be so lucky to have her. Thank you ... Amen.* He sniffed back a few tears, kissed Danyella's cheek, and fell asleep with the hope that a greater power had heard his request.

The next day at work, Kiki seemed to be in a chatty mood. The boring hum in the office was a mismatch for Kiki's energetic spirit. Danyella arrived at work to find an extra-long list of patient verifications to handle. She loved a good challenge, so she focused on her duties and lost a sense of time as she was calling insurance companies and doctors' offices.

In the early afternoon, Danyella suspected that Kiki would pop up over the cubicle wall any minute and drag her into a fun conversation. Kiki was very good at that, and Danyella loved the fun things they chatted about. It was almost as if Danyella had counted down in command to Kiki popping up above the cubicle wall.

"OK, I know you're busy, Danyella, but I have something to tell you!"

"Yeah, I could use a tea break. Let's go to the kitchen."

Joining each other in the hall, Kiki whispered loudly, "OK, so you know Heather in accounting, right?"

"Yes."

"She told me a story this morning that reminded me of you. She opened up to me about her pregnancy struggles she's been experiencing this year," Kiki said, wide-eyed.

"I never knew she struggled with getting pregnant," Danyella said empathetically.

"Yeah, I guess she and her husband had been trying for a while. The first time they got pregnant several years ago, she lost her baby, and so as she was telling me this story, I thought of you." Kiki said as if leading up to something better.

Danyella smiled and nodded at Kiki while filling their cups with hot water from the electric tea kettle.

"Well, about three months ago, she finds out she's pregnant! They are of course over the moon, but when they did the due date testing at the ultrasound, it traced her conception date back to her original due date!" Kiki's expression was full of energy. She stared at Danyella with her eyebrows raised, a big grin, and her head tilted as if she were waiting for Danyella to fill in the rest of the story.

Feeling a little confused by her friend's facial expressions, Danyella said, "That's awesome! I'm so happy for her!" with sincere cheer in her tone.

"I know, but *hello!* You immediately came to mind when I was listening to her story because I know you and John celebrated your baby's due date yesterday with a special dinner. But the question is, did you have sex afterward?"

Danyella laughed and finally understood what Kiki was so excited about. She paused a moment because she loved torturing Kiki with this kind of fun anticipation. "Yes we did!" Danyella finally blurted out with a laugh.

"Oh my gosh! You're pregnant! That's what this whole thing means! Because why in the world would Heather from accounting open up like that to me? We're not that close!"

"Maybe I am. I mean, we really just enjoyed ourselves last night. It wasn't trying like we normally do. And you know what they say when you don't try?" Danyella said while blushing.

"They say you get pregnant!" Kiki said dramatically and with a laugh. A strong dose of excitement filled the air as they walked back to their desks. Danyella felt good believing she was pregnant.

But Kiki was wrong; October's visit from Mother Nature came just as it did every month. That time, Danyella held back the tears and stated her affirmation just as she had planned: *I'm thankful for my period because it means I have the ability to make a baby.* She stated it several times till she felt some relief.

CHAPTER 6

A CHRISTMAS WISH

With the freshness of the winter season, Danyella felt renewed and ready for a new chapter. A few days into December, Danyella noticed that her period hadn't shown up as expected. She jumped out of bed, grabbed her phone, and scrolled through her period tracker app. *I should have had my period three days ago!* Her mind started to go wild with exciting thoughts; she began to think of ways she could reveal a pregnancy to John, and she imagined what it would be like to share the good news with her parents on Christmas Day. Being pregnant was so far from her expectations in reality, but it felt so fun to imagine it as a true possibility.

That day while at work, Danyella found it impossible to focus. She was in baby dreamland imagining how her pregnancy might go and what she would look like with a bulging belly. She was thrilled to be dreaming again.

When John walked through the door that evening, Danyella couldn't hide her excitement. He didn't even have time to ask her what before she blurted out, "I think we're pregnant!"

"Are you sure?" he asked.

"I haven't tested or anything yet, but I'm *never* late, and I'm three days late!"

"Are you going to take a test?"

"I'm kind of nervous about that, but I know I must be pregnant because I'm never late!"

John had no words for his joy. He grabbed Danyella and hugged her.

After dinner, the two sat in the living room nervously waiting for the two minutes till they could rush back into the bathroom and see the results of the test.

"This is so exciting, huh?" Danyella asked.

"Nerve-racking is more like it," John replied.

"But how fun that we're getting to plan a pregnancy together! Most babies these days are accidental. How lucky is our baby that we're hovering over a pregnancy test to find out if we get to start our journey with him or her?"

"This baby is *very* lucky, honey. It already has such an amazing mom!"

"And dad," Danyella added with a smile. "Now let's go see what the test says."

John had been right; walking to the bathroom was nerve-racking. John stood at the door waiting to see the results in Danyella's expression. Her joyful expression quickly faded, and John's heart sank; he didn't need to see the results to know they weren't positive.

"How could this be?" Danyella asked softly.

"It's OK, honey." John rushed to her side to comfort her.

"But it doesn't make any sense. If I'm not pregnant, then where's my period?" she complained while brushing off his attempts to comfort her.

No explanation John could give would help in this situation, so he just rubbed her shoulders and pulled her in for a hug.

"I don't care what this test says. I'm pregnant!" Danyella demanded.

On the fifth day of her no-period streak, cramps set in, and by the afternoon, she was wearing a pad. "I really thought I was pregnant," Danyella whined as Kiki listened intently.

"Maybe this all happened for a reason," Kiki said, sounding like Danyella normally did when giving her advice during tough times. "I mean, think about it … Maybe this is all just setting you up for something better,"

"Better than having my baby here with me right now?" Danyella shot back a little hastier than she meant to. She felt guilty for snapping at her friend, who was just trying to comfort her. A moment of silence … Kiki was looking down …

"You're right!" Kiki said. "*Nothing's* better than being with your baby as soon as possible. But I promise you that there is purpose in your pain. I don't know what it is, but everything has a purpose. You'll eventually find beauty in this long journey you're on."

Danyella's tears started to flow as she listened to Kiki's much-needed advice. Kiki turned at the sound of Danyella's sniffles and quickly wrapped her arms around her sulking friend. Thoughts of what more to say next to heal her friend raced through Kiki's mind as they hugged.

"You want to hear what you would tell me if I were going through this?" Kiki asked.

"Sure."

"You'd say that everything happens for a reason. You'd also say that not everyone gets a chance to spend so much time focusing on their desires. The long journey will make the fruit at the end of this journey so much sweeter. You've been blessed with the opportunity to find beauty in the depths of your despair. Right now, you're at a low, but as your closest friend, I'm blown away by how you've seemed to pick yourself up and keep going with a smile throughout these incredible challenges."

Kiki grabbed her friend's hands and tightened her grip as if to say, *I love you!* Danyella smiled and wiped her tears. She exhaled the heaviness weighing on her heart. She knew Kiki was right, but for the moment, Danyella wanted to grieve.

On Christmas Eve, Danyella couldn't help but ponder what it would have been like to be with her baby. She dreamed of baby pajamas in Christmas colors and silly baby bums on holiday cards and having the best present in the world in her arms. It was a delightful string of dreams. She felt comforted when she allowed her mind to run free with how her desires might have played out.

John's kiss on her forehead interrupted her daydreaming. He handed her a glass of red wine and sat next to her on the couch. The Christmas tree lights sparkled on her glass and twinkled in John's dark eyes. His black hair and mocha skin seem to glow as he grinned and raised his glass in the air.

"Let's toast," he said.

Danyella gazed at her handsome husband. "Toasting just the two of us?"

"Yes. It's Christmas Eve, and I'm feeling grateful and in the holiday spirit," he said charmingly.

Danyella smiled at the subtle yet romantic moment.

"Cheers to another holiday with my beautiful wife, who is already the best mom in the world for my future children. I know it hasn't been easy, but as my wife always says, if it were easy, it wouldn't be fun."

They laughed as they clinked their glasses. Their love could have been felt miles away as they enjoyed each other's company. Their love felt as pure as magic that evening. *Maybe even Santa heard my Christmas wish,* she thought.

Returning to work after the holiday, Danyella felt renewed. Alone at her desk early that morning, she felt the loving energy of her baby by her side. Starting a mental conversation, she said, *I'm sorry Mommy has been sad lately. I miss you, and I've been trying my hardest to be patient, but I'm very impatient!*

Before she heard her daughter's response, she heard, "Hi, Danyella!" It was Karen, who had started on Danyella's team a few weeks earlier. She was bubbly and kind, and she seemed to have taken a liking to Danyella.

"Hi, Karen. How are you?"

"I'm doing great! Well, super great actually! I just discovered some exciting news that I couldn't wait to tell you," Karen said as she beamed with joy.

"What's up?" Danyella replied eagerly.

Karen pulled a picture out of the stack of papers in her hands and handed it to Danyella. It was a picture of Karen and what seemed to be her husband holding a onesie emblazoned with the words Coming June!

"Oh my gosh you're pregnant!" Danyella said trying to sound as joyful as she could while hushing the sounds of confusion. Danyella hadn't known Karen that long, so it came as a mild shock that she was sharing her news so early. Nonetheless, she felt honored that Karen had done so.

"I've just been bursting with joy to share my good news!"

"That explains why you've been glowing so much lately. Congrats!" Danyella said as she hugged Karen. For the first time, the news of someone's pregnancy felt nice even though it wasn't hers.

Danyella watched Karen joyfully bounce back to the other side of the office while she felt a mix of emotions. *What a blessing! But why'd she share this news with me so soon? We've only just met.* But then she heard, *you are next!* She could feel her daughter's excitment. Danyella wanted to believe her, but the last year had left her feeling jaded. She feared that being too optimistic would burn her as it had so many times. But she knew in her heart that her feelings always led her to the right place, so instead of overthinking the matter, she let the good news for her friend's new journey fill her heart and mind.

New Year's Eve brought Danyella and John a desire for a new way of life. They took a break from trying for a baby. Christmas Eve had been so romantic and unplanned that it reminded them that they missed the spontaneity and pleasure of romantic sex, something they had lost in their quest to produce a result. They were ready to release the large burden that transformed sex into a production rather than a pleasure. She felt inspired moving in this new direction and looking at this journey in a new way. New Year's Eve symbolized a new beginning. She was ready to move on from the previous year's pain and suffering.

They decided to ring in the new year at a party with friends. Arriving at the impressive house on a hill overlooking the city, she looked down at her bright-blue cocktail dress and matching shoes nervously wondering if she had picked the right outfit.

"You look amazing, honey!" John said reading her insecure expression.

"Thank you!" She blushed still feeling worried. Her worry faded as soon as she saw her cousins Christy and Abigail. The three started chatting, laughing, and complimenting one another while the men played poker and cussed.

"How does it feel to be out without the baby for the first time?" Danyella asked Christy.

"It's strange. I almost decided not to come tonight. She is only two months old, but my mom was thrilled to get to watch her so I got myself dressed and made it out."

"It must have been hard to leave her for the first time," Danyella said trying to imagine what it would be like to be in her cousin's shoes. She would have taken staying home cuddling with a baby over an evening out with a bunch of drunk adults any night, but she was selfishly thankful that her cousin had made it out to enjoy the evening with her.

"Yes, but being a new mom is way different than I ever imagined," Christy said.

Danyella wished she knew firsthand what Christy was talking about. Instead, she listened intently to her cousin's experience and reveled in at least hearing about motherhood, which made motherhood feel nearer.

Laughs and conversation filled Danyella's ears until one of her favorite songs began to play, changing the energy in the busy room—an energy that made Danyella want to dance. Danyella loved dancing, so she made her way to the dance floor without John, who was busy at the poker tables. She didn't mind that he was gambling, and she also knew he wasn't the dancing type. She just couldn't resist letting her body move when she heard a good song.

As Danyella began to dance, others were inspired and followed her lead. And those who weren't dancing began to watch. She lit up the entire room as she moved. Lost in the beat of the song and the motion of her body, Danyella almost didn't sense the unfamiliar touch of one of Christy's friends dancing with her. Turning to see who had joined her, she saw a man smiling joyfully as he moved with her. His all-white Gucci suit complemented his dark-almond skin. His beautiful jet-black hair and Asian eyes made Danyella feel oddly nervous. She smiled bashfully as he moved in closer while they danced. She wasn't used to being this close to any man other than John. It made her slightly uncomfortable, but she felt an odd familiarity at the same time.

Danyella had met this distant friend only a few times prior. She didn't know him well; he normally was quiet around her, and his excited energy struck her as out of character for him. The song ended, and she exited the dance floor bashfully and joined the women for their typical gossip and laughter.

The separate groups of men and women had kept Danyella and John apart for most of the evening, so when she heard music signaling the countdown, she searched the crowded room for John. "Ten! ... Nine! ..." people were shouting. "Eight! ... Seven! ..." His dark-chocolate eyes met her deep-blues from across the room. They stared at one another as he made his way to her. "Six! ... Five! ..." Danyella's lips widened. She skipped a breath. He still could make her feel like the luckiest girl in the room. "Four! ... Three! ..." There was no one more handsome than her John. He finally made his way to her side. "Two! ... One! ... Happy New Year!" John and Danyella just smiled at one another, a secret facial expression that signaled they had read each other's minds—*Let's get out of here!* With smiles and romance on their faces, they scurried like schoolchildren to the door.

Danyella's short evening dress made the sharp wind unbearable as they ran to their car. Neither of them knew where they were going, but they felt the rush of their romantic exit.

"Where should we go?" Danyella asked, out of breath, once in the car.

"I don't know. Maybe watch the fireworks by the waterfront?"

"That sounds nice!"

They talked and laughed the entire drive. She couldn't remember the last time they'd had so much fun just the two of them. *He really is my best friend*, she thought as he laughed uncontrollably at her jokes.

John parked the car alongside the river road, and they nestled in for the fireworks show. To Danyella's surprise, he turned around and grabbed a bottle of champagne and two glasses from behind his seat.

"Did you plan this?" Danyella asked in an astonished tone.

"I wish I could say I had, but I forgot it in the car on our way to Shelly's and Dave's tonight. I guess I just got lucky leaving it in the car."

"Maybe your soul planned it, which is good enough for me."

She screamed as John popped the cork, and they burst out laughing. He swiftly poured the overflowing liquid into the narrow glasses while giggling.

"I think it's my turn to make the New Year's toast," John said with a wink. "This has been the hardest year I've ever experienced by far, but in some ways, it's been the most beautiful. I guess what I am trying to say is … This not having a baby so easily thing has made me realize how much I really want one … How much I really want one with you. Our baby, whenever he or she comes, will be so lucky to have a mom like you." John paused as Danyella blushed. "Most people have to meet someone before they love and care for them the way you do. But you love this baby to the ends of the earth and back already. I'm looking forward to watching you two love each other forever. So here's to our new year. May it bring many blessings and the chance to meet our baby."

Danyella smiled as tears welled up in her eyes. She was so moved by her husband's loving words. It was like viewing a small window into how her best friend felt about the emotional roller-coaster they had been on together. John was a quiet man who rarely expressed his feelings adequately, but his thoughtful words made her feel that he was indeed joining her on her path that had previously felt so lonely. She realized she hadn't been alone through all the pain like she had previously felt. She was at a loss for words. She leaned in for a kiss. The clink of their glasses chased away all her pain. She knew she was embarking on a new path, and she heard her daughter say, *All's well, Mom. All is always well.*

On January 19, Danyella woke up with the urge to check her phone. Nothing was on the screen. No notifications, no calendar updates, no emails ... She was momentarily perplexed. *OK, baby girl, tell me what I'm supposed to be looking for here.* That was when her eyes caught her ovulation app. She intuitively opened it, and her eyes widened as she saw that her period was late again that month. *Two months in a row? What does this mean?* She felt a mix of emotions—possibly a sign her baby was on the way. She hushed her excitement as she remembered the letdown of last month, but she found it hard to contain her anticipation. *OK, OK, OK, baby! Your day is coming up in three days. If I haven't had my period by then, I'll take a pregnancy test. What a joyous day it would be to find out that we are pregnant on the twenty-second ... Not to mention how symbolic it would be!* Danyella looked up toward the sky in praise.

Those three days felt longer than normal to Danyella, but they were filled with an excitement she kept to herself. The morning of January 22, Danyella didn't even need her alarm. She felt such thrill and enthusiasm for the day that she jumped out of bed, ran to the bathroom mirror, squealed in delight at her reflection, and unwrapped a pregnancy test. The memory of negative tests plagued her, but she swallowed the knot in her throat and tried to shake off the past. She followed the steps and placed the pregnancy stick on the top of the toilet tank, where she had placed so many before. She felt different this time; she finally felt free from the prison of needing an outcome to be a certain way to feel good. She knew she had her baby with her no matter the results.

Danyella made a needless trip to the kitchen for a glass of water just to ease her nerves and distract her mind. At the kitchen sink, she caught a glimpse of the sun making its way up over the landscape and through the window. *How beautiful!* she thought as she gazed into the light. *The next few moments might change my life!* She felt good about embracing a beautiful possibility. Years, even months earlier, she would have been too stressed to notice a beautiful sunrise. She felt so thankful for having found peace.

Walking back to the bathroom, she reminded herself to smile. She felt so confident that she had almost forgotten to show some enthusiasm. With that thought came a sharp sting of guilt for how her baby must have felt knowing she wasn't showing as much excitement as she had the first time, but she brushed the silly thought aside and opened the bathroom door. Her eyes focused on the pregnancy test, and her previous thoughts and feelings melted away; she started to giggle. The test confirmed what Danyella had wanted to feel so many times before. *I'm pregnant! This is where I'm meant to be! This is what I have been longing for my whole life!* She was in a state of absolute bliss.

Keeping the secret to herself for a whole day made Danyella anxious to get home and surprise John with the good news. She had prepared a gift-wrapped box to deliver the test results in. And as if by magic, that night was already their previously arranged date night, so John and Danyella had already planned on going out to dinner at their favorite restaurant in town.

She was so bubbly with anticipation that she could hardly wait for the waitress to finish taking their order. The moment the waitress walked away, Danyella grabbed John's hands and said, "I have an early Valentine's Day gift for you."

"You do?"

"I didn't want you to feel like you had to get me something big, so I wanted to give you your Valentine's Day present early. I've been creating it for a while."

She handed John the thoughtfully wrapped box; he smiled and shook the box to hear what might be inside. "It's light," he noted. He opened the box, and his expression changed from a smile to bewilderment. "Oh my gosh! Are you pregnant?"

"No," Danyella replied jokingly. "Yes of course!" she squealed.

With tears in his eyes, he leaned way over the table and hugged her. They felt each other's overwhelming happiness. It was joy, a thrill, and relief at the same time. They said nothing; tears filled their eyes as they smiled and held hands. Danyella felt that she would never forget this precious moment.

That week, Danyella had a familiar feeling of sureness about her future. She had faith that everything always did work out exactly the way it was supposed to. She felt the sureness of her well-being and knew she was exactly at the right place and doing the right thing at the right time. She had never felt better.

CHAPTER 7

A THANKFUL PREGNANCY

Danyella woke up extra early the next morning; she felt as if someone had woken her up. She laid in bed with the feeling she was supposed to be doing something important. As much as she wanted to stay under the warm covers and wrap her arms around her snoring husband, she knew that when she denied her intuition, her callings would find only louder ways to prove their necessity. It was much easier for her to follow her inner guidance than to hush it only to end up with more dramatic scenarios that would lead her to the same guidance anyway.

She got up and left the bedroom. The hallway seemed unusually cold, so she returned for her robe. Approaching the living room window, she saw a white glow. She smiled and walked a little faster to the window. *What could that bright glow be?* She felt a sense of magic at the sight of the neighborhood covered in snow so thick that it made the walnut trees look alive again. There were no tire tracks or footprints yet. In the silence of the winter morning, she cozied up on her living room floor facing the window and began to meditate.

As the small city of Vancouver woke to the magic of the year's first snowfall, everyone and everything seemed to come to a halt. No buses, no business, and that meant no going to work ... a day all to themselves to do whatever they desired.

She went back to the bedroom and woke John by jumping in bed and throwing her arms around him as she tangled herself up in the blankets. John smiled while keeping his eyes closed. He was usually long gone to work by the time she got up for the day.

"Morning, honey," she said softly as she kissed his cheek.

"Morning, my pregnant wife," he said with a smile. Hearing John call her his pregnant wife felt so good.

"Get up, sleepyhead. I'll make you breakfast," Danyella said.

"What time is it? Do you have time before I have to leave for work?"

"I doubt you'll be going to work today, honey. Take a look outside. You're all mine!" she said as she giggled. John opened his eyes, slid out of bed, and went to the window. He grinned at the sight of nature giving him a day off with his wife.

Danyella cooked breakfast and the smell of bacon filled the air. She felt her mouth fill up with saliva and her stomach start to turn. She ran to the sink to execute her first harsh experience with morning sickness. Her last pregnancy had made her feel queasy at times, but she had never felt the urge to puke—until now. She caught her breath and thought, *Thank you, baby, for this morning sickness ... I'm so thankful you're here!* She smiled as she wiped her chin and drank some water to rehydrate.

From that day forward, she treated every morning sickness episode with the same grateful chant. She was so thankful for this life inside her and for getting to experience another pregnancy. Even the so-called worst parts seemed to be filled with love and happiness for her. She was welcoming it all into her experience with open arms.

For the first few weeks, she didn't see the number twenty-two around as often as normal. It was as if her daughter were on vacation. She didn't pay much attention to the absence of her daughter's daily hellos; instead, she turned her attention to the fun she was having, including daydreaming about baby showers and nursery decorating. There were so many fun and exciting new things that came along with being pregnant. Baby thoughts occupied her mind's airtime approximately 77 percent of the day. She was thrilled to be dreaming about it all.

Three months went by in a blink of an eye, and Danyella finally started to tell others about her pregnancy; their reactions varied. Some were extremely excited, almost jumping for joy. Others seemed to be fearful of being happy about something they couldn't wrap their arms around yet. That bothered Danyella at first, but shortly, what seemed to have bothered her before only focused her on what she really wanted—to live life to the fullest even if she might lose. To treat every day as if it were the best day she would ever live. To enjoy this baby to the fullest no matter what tomorrow brought.

That Friday after a long day of work at the office, Danyella sluggishly walked up her apartment steps. John opened the door before she had time to turn the handle. "Are you feeling a little tired today, honey?" he asked.

"Yeah. I'm not sure if I got enough sleep last night. I'm really tired."

"Let's go out to dinner then. How about our Vietnamese place down the street?"

"That sounds great, babe," Danyella said in relief. All she could think about was cuddling up in bed early, so a quick dinner out sounded like a lifesaver.

At the restaurant, she felt an urge to run to the restroom. An older woman with white hair and crystal-blue eyes was exiting the bathroom stall as Danyella walked in. The woman gave Danyella a sweet smile that felt so warm and comforting that the feeling lingered with her as she sat down in the stall. *Do I know her?* The thought of the woman vanished as her attention quickly shifted to the sight of blood on her underwear. A sharp stab of fear surged through her body. Her mind raced through the memories of her previous miscarriage. With the pain of the past plaguing her mind, she almost forgot to breathe. *How could this be happening again? All is well … All is well … All is well.* Danyella tried to calm down. She left the restroom and sat across the table from John, who was busy examining the menu. When he finally looked up, Danyella could no longer hold in her tears.

"Honey, what's wrong?"

"I'm bleeding again, honey!" she replied in a quaky voice.

"Did it just start? Let's call your doctor."

He didn't give her time to answer the first question; he pulled out his phone and gave it to her.

With nervous hands, Danyella dialed her doctor's number. The joyful tone in the receptionist's voice seemed to calm Danyella's nerves momentarily as she explained what was going on. Danyella's face turned from extreme panic to pure relief as she spoke to the nurse. Before Danyella could press the end call button, John grabbed her hand. "What did they say, honey?"

"She said she's going to send a hormone prescription to the pharmacy for me to pick up tonight and will also schedule an ultrasound for tomorrow morning to make sure baby's OK." Just saying the plan out loud seemed to shift their energy.

John leaned across the table and kissed her. "It's going to be OK, honey. I can feel it."

Danyella smiled and thought about her desire for her baby's well-being.

The next morning, the ultrasound proved that her growing child was safe and healthy. Danyella had never felt so thankful and relieved. She celebrated by buying an angel figurine at the dollar store across the street from the ultrasound office. Growing up, she had a collection of angel figurines. Maybe it was their well-known symbolism, or maybe it was their beauty, but they always made her feel safe. She kept the new angel on her nightstand as a reminder of the well-being she had felt so abundantly after finding out her baby was safe.

CHAPTER 8

MAYA

Week by week, Danyella's belly grew and grew. She reveled in the feeling of her growing baby's movement. In time, she sensed the familiar signs of her daughter's spirit nearby once again. She was excited to be communicating again in her mind with her daughter as she had before. It was a special relationship that was unexplainable. She knew that most people believed only what they could see, so she was keeping her special relationship with her daughter to herself.

John and Danyella had decided not to find out the sex until birth. That seemed to be a harder task for others than it was for the new parents. She enjoyed the fun guessing games with all her friends and family about the baby being a boy or girl. Her coworkers even started a lottery on their guesses of the gender. She was intrigued by the thought of being able to connect with her baby in such a way that she would have a mother's instinct on what the gender was. Since her first child, who was never born, was a girl, she naturally began to think of the current unborn child as a female.

One afternoon at work, Kiki said, "I had a dream about you and your baby last night!"

Danyella loved hearing Kiki's fascinating dreams, which were usually about the future and always had interesting details.

"Do tell!"

"I remember you were pregnant, but not early pregnant like you are now. Like end of your pregnancy pregnant. I was visiting you at maybe a baby shower. You were telling me you had this labor thing under control. Almost like you were saying, 'Bring it on. I got this.' In the dream I couldn't believe how long your hair was."

Danyella giggled at that; she had just had her hair cut to shoulder length.

"But then a child walked up beside you," Kiki said, "pulled a sucker out of his or her mouth, scrunched up his or her eyes, and said to me, 'Hi, Aunty Kiki!'"

"So I was pregnant with my second child in your dream?" Danyella asked excitedly.

"Yes!"

"Was the first baby a boy or girl?"

"Not sure. Couldn't really tell. The child was maybe two or three and had long, curly, black hair, but the energy felt like a boy."

"So interesting," Danyella said with a smile.

The two could have talked for hours about Kiki's dream. It thrilled them to think it could be a sign of the future.

That night at dinner, Danyella described Kiki's dream in detail to John.

"Wow, what a dream!" John said with more enthusiasm than he actually felt. He was more amused by Danyella's excitement than he was by the dream, but he kept that a secret.

"Do you have a feeling what the baby might be?" a wide-eyed and giddy Danyella asked.

"Not really. I guess I just think of both. You know me. I'm happy with either a boy or a girl, honey. I'm just excited we get one."

"Me too! No matter what we have, it'll be fun."

"So when you imagine it, is it a boy or a girl?"

What a good question! She relaxed, placed her hands on her belly, and closed her eyes. John looked up from his meal and smiled at sight of his wife pondering his question. He adored how she was enjoying all parts of being pregnant. He knew how much it all meant to her.

She opened her eyes. "When I imagine the baby, I see it dancing with me." She giggled. "And it looks like a boy."

"That's two votes for a boy. What about names?"

"OK, so there's something I have to tell you."

"You already told me you're pregnant, so there's not much more you can lay on me."

"How about if I pick the girl's name and you pick the boy's name?"

"Sure!"

She was surprised that he had bought into her plan so quickly.

"When I was thirteen, I picked out a name for a girl that I've saved up. So to be fair, if you let me use my girl name, you can name the boy. Within reason of course."

John shot Danyella a sneaky look. "OK, the boy will be named Jay Z!"

They laughed. She loved the way he always made things fun and lighthearted. She felt time slow down almost like it was going to freeze so she could take a mental photo. She always wanted to remember precious moments like the one they were experiencing.

"So what's your name for a girl?"

"Sofia Jane ..."

"That is beautiful!"

"Really? You mean it? I've wanted to name my daughter that for almost my whole life."

"I love it, honey. It's almost as beautiful as my wife," he said as he leaned over the table to kiss her forehead.

She rubbed her belly. "Did you hear that, baby? If you're a girl, we have your name!"

"And if you are a boy, you are stuck with whatever name I come up with," John joked.

"Are you fond of any boy names?"

"I like Markus."

Danyella wasn't very good at hiding her dissatisfaction for his name idea in her expression. "What about naming our boy after his daddy?" she suggested with a soft smile.

"Name him after me? I like that. But we can call him Jonathan." John beamed.

"I love that, honey. It sounds so perfect."

That night, she tossed and turned beside John, who looked as if he was having the best sleep of his life. *Why can't I fall asleep?* The clock read 10:22. *Hi, baby girl. You can't sleep either? Well, to the kitchen we go.*

She grabbed a light snack and some warm milk and honey. She never knew if her grandma's warm milk and honey mixture actually made her fall asleep or if her grandma had been really good at convincing her it would. Finding a cozy place on the couch, she turned on the TV. She scrolled through the channels looking for something that grabbed her attention. Her finger slowed down on the channel button as she approached channel twenty-two. *Let's see what you have on your channel, baby.* It was some sort of interview with an author. *Baby, are you the intellectual type?*

"Names given at birth are very symbolic, and some might even say that they help dictate parts of the child's personality," the author explained.

We were just talking about names! She raised the volume.

"So does your book go into depth on the relationship of names and their meanings?"

"Yes," the author said, "and it also uncovers the statistics compiled by our thirteen-year study on names and how they affect their owners. We have found that a name is significantly grouped with personality types ..."

Danyella started up a conversation with her daughter as the author went on. She knew that this late-night TV segment on baby names was no coincidence and that her baby was communicating with her in a big way. Danyella groaned at the thought of changing her lifelong dream of a baby name, but she couldn't deny her daughter's request. She knew she needed to take it seriously whether she wanted to or not.

OK, baby girl. This is the deal! Momma knows that names are super important. I'm willing to give up my lifelong name for you, but you have to tell me what name you want. She had been practicing allowing her daughter's responses to flow in, but the responses still seemed a little fuzzy. Danyella couldn't hear them clearly all the time, but she could hear them, which was a start.

She didn't have to wait long before a name floated into her mind as if someone had lightly set it down for her brain to pick it up. "Manda?" Danyella asked. She didn't feel a hundred percent sure about that name, but she was starting to feel sleepy. She knew she would need some rest to make sense of everything. She blew her daughter's spirit a kiss into the air, went back to bed, and snuggled up next to John. She felt good, knowing that the milk and honey had done its job; as soon as she closed her eyelids, she fell asleep.

The next morning, she smiled as she recalled her late-night conversation with her daughter. *What a beautiful relationship we have.* Danyella was already in love with her sweet baby girl. *Or now known as Manda?* She wasn't sure she had gotten the name right; something felt off about it as if someone was tugging on her brain saying, *Close but not quite.* She shrugged off the mind battle and got ready for work.

Walking into the office, Danyella saw Kiki, one of the few people she knew would understand about her mother-daughter conversations. The thought of letting Kiki in on the name secret felt like fun.

"Good morning, gorgeous!" Kiki said.

"*Awww*, thanks, and back at ya, girly! You'll never guess what happened to me last night!"

"I'd like to say that I've had my coffee and could make some sort of psychic guess that would blow your socks off, but you're going to have to settle for me asking, 'What?'"

Danyella lowered her voice and told her about her baby-name adventures.

"Danyella! You're willing to give up Sofia Jane?"

"For my daughter to have the name she desires, which is dramatically important for someone's life purpose, yes, in a heartbeat!"

"I guess if my baby was talking to me as much as your baby talks to you, I'd give up such a perfectly planned name too," Kiki said with a wink. "So what's the new name again? Maya?"

"No. That's so pretty, but the name I thought I heard was Manda."

"That's pretty too."

"Maya ..." Danyella whispered while concentrating on the good feeling she had had when she had first heard that name.

Her concentration was disturbed by her telephone. This intriguing name situation would have to wait. Later that evening, she called her aunt Samantha. She couldn't wait to tell her about all the signs she was experiencing about her future child's spirit. With her aunt Samantha being psychically connected to the world beyond, she knew that her aunt would be thrilled to hear all she was experiencing. Danyella had always found her aunt's spiritual gifts fascinating and had bonded with her in a way that her sister, Jacky, never had; if anyone would understand what she was talking about, it would be her aunt.

"Hello, my dear!"

"Hi, Aunt Samantha! How'd you know it was me?"

"I felt you wanted to talk to me, and then my phone rang. So I knew it was you, honey."

"So much has been happening lately with the baby, Aunt Samantha."

"Has your daughter been talking to you?"

"She has. I asked her the other day if she had a name she preferred, and she told me her name was Manda."

"That's such a beautiful name! I knew a nurse one time named Maya. I always loved her name."

Danyella didn't have the heart to correct her aunt on mishearing the name. But then she remembered Kiki had mentioned Maya as well. *I discounted Kiki's mistake, but this time, I can tell there's something more here. That must be the name! Yes, baby girl! Maya is a beautiful name!* Danyella felt an overwhelming sureness in her discovery. "Yes, it's a beautiful name. I'm thrilled! I'm so connected to her. She's a beautiful part of my life already."

"Yes, but don't get hung up on the baby girl you're so connected to being the one you give birth to this time around. You never know if she's the one growing in you or not."

"You're absolutely right, which leads me to my other stories ..."

They chatted for hours until Danyella yawned, which reminded her to glance at the clock—9:22. She smiled at the sight of her daughter's number. "Aunt Samantha, it's getting late. I better get this baby in my belly off to bed," Danyella said with a chuckle.

"Of course, sweetie!"

They ended the call with warm smiles and love in their hearts. Danyella snuggled into her cozy king-size bed and fell fast asleep.

In her second trimester, Danyella was truly enjoying being pregnant. Feeling her baby tumble and turn was a remarkable experience. She marveled at how something so tiny could move around inside her belly so quickly. The motions were strong and swift; to Danyella, they felt more like a masculine energy. She still felt unsure on the baby's sex, but she truly felt that didn't matter. She was so head over heels in love with being able to bring a life into this world that she didn't care if it was a boy or girl. A baby to love, learn, and enjoy was what she focused on.

CHAPTER 9

TWINS?

On her way home from work one evening, Danyella stopped at the grocery store for the last few ingredients for dinner. The store was experiencing the after-work rush, and the checkout lines were annoyingly long, but she didn't mind; she was enjoying feeling her baby kick. She was glowing as she stood in line holding her belly. Her happiness was bubbling out of her like a joyful fog that seemed to catch the attention of everyone who passed by. People were gazing and smiling at the lovely scene of a mother in love with her baby in her belly. Danyella hardly noticed them; she was too wrapped up in the moment.

"How many are you having?" asked an older woman who stood behind her in the checkout line.

Danyella turned around to see a smiling woman of her mother's age, with short brown hair and glasses.

"Oh! I'm having just one." Danyella blushed and rubbed her belly.

"Are you sure? I'm not saying that you look huge or anything, darlin', but I'm a great-aunt and a grandma of twelve, so I have a good sense about these things. And my senses say that you have more than one baby in there."

"Well, I'm pretty sure ... During my ultrasound, they saw only one peanut." Danyella giggled.

"Well, sometimes, doctors can be wrong," the woman said in confidence with a wink.

Driving home, Danyella couldn't get that conversation off her mind. *Twins?* She chuckled. *Wouldn't that be something?* Her dad's side had had several sets of twins, so it wasn't a big stretch to think it could happen to her. She loved the idea of twins, but she wasn't sure John would feel the same. Regardless, she felt joy in thinking about it.

The next day at work, she went to the cafeteria for lunch rather than eat the leftovers she had brought from home. Everyone walking by her smiled to watch her practically floating down the hallway in joy. She was confident about every decision she'd made lately. She was listening to her inner guidance system and taking action only on things that felt good. Her new strategy seemed to be working. Danyella felt great.

After going through the line, Danyella spotted Kiki at a table in the corner. Kiki's face lit up when she saw Danyella and her pointy belly. "I was hoping I'd find you here."

"I was hiding over here from everyone except you," Kiki said playfully. "How's the angel baby doing in there?"

"Really well! Growing lots. I can't stop eating. I eat almost every hour now."

"I remember I was like that with my twins—always hungry."

"Twins?"

"I don't think I ever told you about my twins. I got pregnant when I was very young, before I was married. They obviously didn't make it. But they're still so dear to my heart. I remember being pregnant with them like it was yesterday." Kiki said with a faraway look in her eyes.

"Wow, Kiki! You never told me that. I lost only one. I can't imagine losing two."

"I'm OK now, but it took a while to get through that. I'll never forget them. Their spirits are with me forever."

"This is the second time the subject of twins has come up recently. I think my angels are trying to tell me something. Yesterday, someone said that she thought I was having twins."

"Interesting. Who?"

"A woman in the checkout line at the grocery store."

"You never know. You're devouring calories like they're going out of style," Kiki said laughing.

Danyella laughed too as she realized she was scarfing down her lunch in between sentences. Both of them pondered the beauty of there possibly being two babies on the way.

That evening when Danyella got home, she smelled dinner and saw the table all set with flickering candles. "Wow! What's this?"

"Just a delicious dinner for my amazing wife, who's doing a great job of carrying my unborn child. Thought it would be a nice surprise to cook for you. And I thought candles would be romantic," John said in a debonair tone.

Danyella beamed with pride. She ran her fingers through his hair and leaned in for a kiss. His pouty brown lips always made her melt. "So what did you make?"

"Your favorite—marinated fish, rice, and tomatoes," John said with a wink.

Her mouth began to water at the mention of the dish. She took her first bite, closed her eyes, and relished the burst of flavors. "I hope our baby will like Asian food like we do." With those words, Danyella felt a jab inside her womb. "Wow!" She giggled. "Our baby just kicked me harder than ever before. It was sort of like he or she was saying, 'Yes, Mom, I will!'"

"Already communicating with us!" John said with a chuckle.

She smiled and thought, *If he only knew, Maya!*

The proud father-to-be spent the rest of the evening rubbing Danyella's belly and asking questions out loud and waiting for a response by the motion of the baby's kick. Danyella felt at home. This was where she always had dreamt she would be. She was truly enjoying this part of her life.

In her third trimester, she had been asked if she was having twins by an overwhelming number of people. She was starting to think that maybe her doctor was missing something. *How's it possible that so many strangers think I'm having twins? And they all seem so sure of it. Is it a sign?* She wasn't sure what this sign meant, but she took the astonishing number of signs as an indication that something charming was occurring.

To Danyella, it didn't matter if she had one or two on the way; she was just thrilled to be experiencing any type of pregnancy. She also wasn't worried about Maya being the baby inside her womb. Danyella felt a strong sureness that Maya would always be a part of her experience, and that felt good enough for her.

Danyella was enjoying getting to know Maya's spirit more and more each day. She began to sense a change in the energy around her body when Maya arrived and exited. All the cells in her body would feel warm and fuzzy. Recognizing Maya's energy was a new skill for Danyella that seemed to come naturally. She loved how often Maya was entering her experience. It felt like a love Danyella had never felt before.

Before Danyella knew it, 9/22—her due date—arrived, but she could tell that her labor was nowhere near. Regardless, she decided to celebrate. Since that day was the beginning of her maternity leave, she slept in and made herself a large breakfast. *I could get used to this lifestyle!* she thought as she cut up fruit to top her fresh waffles. She ate on the porch and watched the squirrels hide their winter meals under the pines. She was mindful about each bite of her breakfast and how many flavors she was tasting. She had noticed that when she took time to focus on the simple but divine details of anything, things seemed utterly perfect. She felt her perfect well-being at times like that. She sensed the beauty the universe offered, even in something as small as her breakfast.

She decided to treat herself to a pedicure. Her favorite songs were playing one after another on the radio when she drove to the salon. She turned the volume up; songs she had heard a thousand times before suddenly sounded so different. She felt a happiness amplifying throughout her entire body. She shortly realized that she was speeding. She giggled as she pressed the brake to slow down. *Oops!*

The nail salon was practically empty; three nail technicians almost stepped over one another to welcome Danyella in the door. One of them told her to pick out her nail polish color while she prepared the footbath. Danyella preferred to scan the colors and wait for one to jump out at her; she did, and the first color that stood out was a pastel baby blue. *Not what I had in mind, but I'll take it.*

The nail technician guided Danyella to her chair. As she scrubbed her feet, she looked at the nail polish and said, "Very pretty! Are you having a boy?"

"I'm not sure what I'm having. We'll have to wait until I give birth."

The woman smiled and nodded.

"You want to know what you're having?" another technician asked. "I can tell you!"

"She doesn't want to know!" Danyella's technician sounded irritated with her coworker.

"I'd be happy with either gender, and I really enjoy all the guessing. It's fun!" Danyella said

"I'm guessing a boy," the third technician said.

"Since you don't want to know, I won't tell you what you're having," the second technician said. "But I've never been wrong!"

That conversation ended, and Danyella read her book while enjoying the massage of the pedicure chair. She hardly noticed the tall, slender woman who had been getting a manicure on the far side of the room make her way to the chair next to her. "So what do you think you're having? A mother's intuition is far more valuable than strangers' guesses or psychic predictions," she said with a wink.

"I'm a little stumped. I've had some strange things happen during my pregnancy that make me unsure. I've had around a hundred people ask me if I was having twins based on just their feelings, but my ultrasound showed only one." Danyella blushed thinking how strange that might have sounded to someone she didn't know. The woman looked shocked, which made Danyella feel even more insecure about what she had shared.

The woman leaned toward Danyella and began to whisper. "While you were talking with those women, my nail tech whispered, 'She's having twins but doesn't know it ... a boy and a girl.' Can you believe that?"

"Really?"

"Yes. I found it odd until you said many others had thought you were having twins."

"Nothing surprises me anymore," Danyella said with a chuckle.

"I wouldn't be surprised if two babies pop out," the woman said with a laugh.

Danyella laughed too; she knew that regardless of how many babies she was having, there was something very mystical about all these twin signs; she wanted to learn what they meant.

That evening when John got home, an antsy Danyella blurted out, "You'll never guess what happened today!"

"Your water broke?" John said half-kidding.

"No, silly! You know how people always think I'm having twins?"

"Yes ...?"

"A nail lady from the salon overheard me talking to the technicians there about the baby's gender, and she told another customer that I'm having twins. The other customer was spooked."

John wasn't fascinated with psychic intuitions and spiritual signs, but he enjoyed watching his wife get so excited about it. "Honey, if two come out, I might pass out. Will you catch me?" John joked.

Danyella laughed; she was just thrilled to have someone to share her tall tale with, even if it didn't thrill John as it did her.

CHAPTER 10

A VERY LONG JOURNEY

The week following her due date felt extremely long to Danyella, who was not the waiting type. She distracted herself by cleaning out all the closets and cabinets and enjoying long naps each afternoon, but those naps made it hard for her to sleep at night. She snuggled into bed next to John earlier than her body was ready to sleep. She turned on the TV to find something new to watch. She scanned the movie section for new arrivals but quickly discovered that the weeklong wait for her baby to arrive had provided her with more TV time than she had realized. She settled for an old romantic comedy instead, which felt oddly fitting.

Halfway through the movie, she felt her stomach grumble. *You hungry, baby? Let's go get a snack.*

She tiptoed back into the bedroom with her snack tray and climbed in bed as cautiously as she could.

John opened his eyes to see what the commotion was on the other side of the bed.

"Sorry, honey. I didn't mean to wake you."

"What are you doing awake, babe?"

"I haven't been able to sleep lately."

"You should get some rest, honey."

"You're right. After I eat my snack, I'll get some shut-eye, promise."

John pulled himself up to reach for a kiss, turned over, and quickly fell back asleep. Danyella ate her snack while watching the movie, but it wasn't long before her eyes felt heavy, and she drifted off to sleep too.

Danyella woke up to a strange feeling at the bottom of her belly. She sat up to check if her water had broken. The bed didn't feel damp, but her mind urged her to go to the bathroom. Danyella looked at the clock; it was early morning, and John was still sound asleep. She got up and hobbled to the bathroom. The strange feeling became more intense. As she stepped into the bathroom, a gush of water hit the floor, which shocked her even though she knew that would eventually happen. *OK ... Here we go, baby!* She grabbed the base of her belly. "John?" She tried not to sound scared so he wouldn't be frightened.

John stumbled into the hallway with his eyes barely open and found Danyella cleaning the bathroom floor with a towel. "What happened, honey?" John asked with a yawn.

"My water broke!" Danyella said with a smile.

John smiled. He was calmer than she had expected he'd be, waking up to find her in the early stages of labor.

Her contractions were light and far apart; she knew she had time before her labor would speed up. She called her midwife and tried to settle down to follow the advice she had heard so many times before: "Get some rest in the early stages of labor." *But who am I kidding? I can't rest, let alone sleep—I'm too excited!*

John was pacing the living room and the kitchen pretending to straighten things up. "Maybe we should call your mom and sister?"

"It's pretty early for that. It's only three o'clock. We'll have quite a while before things start really happening."

But that didn't convince John. She saw discomfort written all over his face. "How about we give them till the morning or until something new happens, babe?"

With a relieved nod of his head, he agreed to her suggestion, and they settled on the couch to watch a movie.

But as soon as the sun began to rise, John couldn't wait a moment longer, and he quickly dialed his mother-in-law's number. Danyella saw that he was having a harder time than she had anticipated. Her thoughts were interrupted by another contraction that started to rise, making her wince and clutch the base of her belly with both of her hands. She began to lose her focus on John and concentrated on breathing through the pain, just as her birthing instructor had advised.

A few contractions passed before her mom's and sister's smiling faces walked through the front door. "Hi, honey! How are you holding up?" Danyella's mom asked as she made her way to Danyella and began rubbing her back. Danyella was relieved to have her mother and sister in the room. She called her midwife team every few hours to update them; the contractions were still far apart but seemed to be getting stronger.

Danyella had studied every birthing book, birthing video, and birthing class she could get her hands on, but nothing had prepared her for the pain involved; she clenched each time a contraction began. Her midwife's instructions were, "Let your body go limp like a noodle." She tried that, but it was harder to do than she had expected.

Around dinner time, Mandy, her midwife, and Cammy, Mandy's assistant, arrived and began to set things up for her home birth. The apartment was smaller than most of the houses they were used to delivering babies in, so the midwives set the blue circular birthing tub up in the dining room; it was the size of a four-person hot tub. They ran a hose from the kitchen sink to fill it, and the sound of running water helped Danyella relax between contractions.

She was thrilled to have more female company, especially ones who would track her progress and who could tell her how far along she was. Even small things, like having her vitals taken, seemed to break up the agony of waiting for another contraction.

Mandy checked Danyella's cervix but couldn't hide the look of disappointment on her face. "You're only one and a half centimeters dilated."

"Wow … I'm not as far along as I thought."

"First-time births usually take longer to dilate, so this is normal," Cammy reassured her. "You can do a few things to speed it up."

Speeding things up definitely appealed to Danyella. She was ready to work toward the end of her pain, even if it meant increasing it at first.

"Walk up and down the stairs," Mandy suggested.

Danyella began to march on the stairs outside her apartment in between contractions. She was determined to do whatever it took to get closer to cuddling with her newborn baby.

Danyella almost couldn't contain her squeals of joy a few hours later when Mandy checked her cervix and reported that she had dilated four more centimeters. Her contractions were becoming more intense. Her family and the midwives were getting tired; the women were taking shifts supporting Danyella and napping, but Danyella's mother stuck by her daughter's side, despite how tired she was; she sat by the birthing tub and eased Danyella's thoughts about the pain. Danyella felt so lucky to have her mom with her; she could make her feel better just by a single word or touch.

In the midst of her pain, Danyella's mind raced with questions. *This is how everybody comes to earth? Mothers do this over and over? This is the most painful experience ever! Why all the pain?* Danyella wanted to scream her thoughts out loud, but she was too tired and in too much pain to talk.

When another contraction started, she got up on her knees, grabbed the birthing tub's handles, and rocked side to side in a circular motion to help her cope with the intense pain. At the peak of that contraction, Danyella thought, *I'll* never *do this again!*

When morning came, Danyella began to feel overwhelmed by the pain and the idea she had been at it for over twenty-four hours with little progress. She mustered the courage to speak her mind. "This doesn't make sense! This doesn't seem right! When are things going to happen?"

"What do you mean, Danyella?" Mandy asked in an annoyingly calm tone.

"Why hasn't anything happened yet? I feel like my body isn't transitioning to the next step. Why?" Danyella pleaded as she began to cry.

"First-time births can take a while. Would you like us to check your cervix and see how far you've progressed?"

Danyella nodded vigorously and got in position, lying on her back with her knees bent and opened wide. She began to breathe steadily and offered a mental prayer to keep her thoughts from running wild. But even her prayer couldn't hold back the emotions inspired by her extreme exhaustion. Tears fell onto the towel she was lying on.

Mandy's face flushed with concern. "You said you'd had a cervix biopsy when you were younger, right?"

"Yes, in my early twenties."

"There's a lot of scarring on your cervix, and I think that's making it hard to soften. I'll massage it to help it relax."

"How far along am I?"

"You haven't dilated any farther from last night, which concerns me a little. But we'll see if massaging helps, OK? We'll see in an hour if it helped any. If there's no progression, let's talk about possibly transferring to the hospital instead of having the baby at home, as originally planned."

Danyella nodded; she tried not to focus on a birth different from what she had desired. But with a plan in place, Danyella felt a boost of faith. She continued to work through contractions while her birthing team ate breakfast. They offered bites to Danyella, but all she could stomach was liquids.

The sun was rising; it looked like a beautiful day outside. Danyella kept her eyes on the clock. As soon as an hour had passed, she stood up and walked to the towel on the ground where her midwives had previously checked her cervix. The determined look on her face told her midwives that Danyella wasn't going to politely ask for another exam; she was showing everyone that she was ready to be checked again.

As Mandy checked her cervix, disappointed looks washed over her midwives' faces. "No change," Mandy said.

"Let's go to the hospital!" Danyella blurted out, which was exactly what John had wanted to hear her say and what he had wanted to scream so many times since he'd woken up to find his pregnant wife in so much pain and distress. Everyone looked relieved as they bustled around, getting things ready to go.

When Danyella got up from the floor, she felt a warm stream of blood trickling down both of her legs. Her face went white as she saw the bright-red blood flow from her body. She quickly looked up at Mandy for direction.

"I think your cervix is bleeding from when I loosened it up. It was really scarred. Let's get you to the hospital." She grabbed her phone and called to prepare for Danyella's transfer.

Everyone packed up what they needed and rushed to their vehicles. Jacky rode in the back seat with Danyella while John drove. The car ride seemed to be a distraction that slowed down the speed of her contractions; the freeway was clogged with rush-hour traffic that made it seem like a parking lot. Danyella tried to stay positive, but she was dreading having the next contraction in a sea of onlookers in the neighboring cars scrunched so closely together. She grabbed Jacky's hand as she felt another contraction set in. Since there was no room to move, the only thing she could do was scream.

Wrapped up in the pain of her contractions, she lost the concern for who was around. It felt good to scream.

"It's just like the movies!" John said with a laugh, which lightened the mood and made Danyella smile after her contraction ended too.

The thirty-minute car ride felt like several hours with the stop-and-go of heavy traffic. Soon, the embarrassing car ride came to an end when they arrived at the hospital; John pulled into the lane closest to the lobby door and turned on his hazard lights. Danyella quickly exited the car and sped through the hospital lobby; she was determined to get to the maternity wing before another contraction hit. Jacky followed with Danyella's bag, trying to keep up with her sister's quick pace.

A volunteer saw the two women coming and tried to offer Danyella a wheelchair, but she blew right past him; Jacky thanked the volunteer and accepted the help. Jacky chased after her sister with the wheelchair. "Danyella, sit! I'll push you there. It'll be much faster!"

Danyella hesitated in fear of another contraction hitting, but her people-pleasing tendencies urged her to comply. As her bottom hit the firm seat of the wheelchair, a sharp contraction set in, rippling pain throughout her entire body and prompting her to yell, "*Cooonnnnttttrrrracctiiiiooon!*" Everyone in the lobby turned in her direction; a few laughed and others smiled knowing what Danyella was going through. Her pain heavily outweighed her embarrassing moment.

Once safely on the second floor, they checked in to the Maternity Department, and she was taken to her birthing room. The nurses promptly administered pitocin and an epidural to ease the pain. Danyella finally felt relief. She took a deep breath and relaxed as her nerves unwound. She felt exhausted. The nurse reclined the bed and suggested that Danyella get some shut-eye. Danyella was too tired to say a single word; she just smiled and nodded. The last thing she saw before she closed her tired eyes was her relieved husband smiling as he sat in an oversized chair in the corner of the room.

Three hours later, Danyella woke up. She felt strong and confident again; she saw her husband, her mom, and her sister focused on her. "Did you get some good rest, honey?" John asked. Danyella nodded, smiled, and stretched her arms.

A nurse walked in and smiled to see Danyella awake and feeling good. "Glad to see you got some sleep, sweetie. I'll let the doctor know you're awake. She'll come check on you."

"Thank you!" Danyella said in an optimistic tone. She was more than ready to start pushing. Her body was mildly numb due to the epidural, but she could tell it was time.

The doctor came in, examined Danyella, and announced, "You're fully dilated! It's time to start pushing!"

Excitement filled the room. John squeezed her hand in support and joy. "By dinner, you'll have a baby!" Danyella's mom said.

"Hopefully!" Jacky chimed in with a tone of skepticism.

Danyella began to push with perseverance. She discovered that there was a learning curve to this new skill that wasn't coming naturally due to the numbness caused by the epidural. Push after push, Danyella began to catch on. She felt some minor indications that she was making progress.

After a few hours of pushing, a small head with jet-black hair started appearing at the opening. The women clapped and marveled at how long the baby's hair was. The midwives brought in a mirror for Danyella to see what they were so excited about. This new milestone inspired her to keep going. She looked at the monitor as a new contraction began to set in. She prepared her breath for another hard push.

Dinnertime passed, and Danyella was still pushing. She was making progress but slowly. She started feeling tired again. The monitor noted a drop in her baby's heart rate. Danyella knew something wasn't right; she called for the doctor. "I'm tired, and I don't feel there's been much progress. What's the next step?" Danyella asked feeling defeated.

"You've been pushing way longer than most people push. Four hours of pushing has been long enough in my opinion. I think we need to get ready for a C-section," Dr. Jay said.

"Is there something that comes before a C-section?" Danyella pleaded.

"We can try a vacuum, but I want to prep for a C-section because you get only three pushes with the vacuum. If it isn't successful, we'll have to take you to surgery."

Danyella agreed to the plan, and shortly, the room filled with nurses and trays of medical instruments and dark-blue medical paper. Danyella took a deep breath and got ready for her three strong pushes. The epidural had started to wear off; she felt her body getting ready for another contraction. Dr. Jay positioned the vacuum on the baby's exposed crown.

"I need to push now!" Danyella announced.

"OK. Let's give the first push a go!" Dr. Jay announced to the medical team behind her.

Danyella looked at John, Jacky, and her mom, who were huddled on the side of the room, and she saw their expressions of fear. She closed her eyes. In her mind, time seemed to slow down. Danyella took a deep breath and pushed with all her might. At the end of the push, a loud *Pop!* startled her and caused Jacky to scream in terror.

"The noise was only lost suction, everyone. It's OK! This baby has so much hair that the vacuum lost suction," Dr. Jay announced.

Everyone in the room took a deep breath and waited for the next contraction to swell.

"Here comes push two!" Danyella said, grabbing her knees to prepare for the push. Dr. Jay was ready. She took a deep breath and pushed with all the strength she had left. The baby came down a lot farther but not out. *Please oh please help my baby come out on this next push! Help my baby to be safe!* she prayed. Danyella felt calmness sweep over her. She knew her angels had heard her prayer. She was again confident that it would all work out the way it was supposed to. She felt her body bearing down.

Dr. Jay saw the look in her eyes and the tension in her body. "Here's our third and final push, everyone. Get ready!"

They all held their breath. Danyella closed her eyes and pushed with all her might. She felt a sudden release of pressure. She opened her eyes and saw her baby soaring through the air in Dr. Jay's grasp. The pressure and force it had taken to pull the baby out had sent the newborn straight up in the air. Her eyes caught sight of his genitals. *It's a boy!* Her heart warmed. His face was the most perfect thing she had ever seen. His tan skin appeared purple and breathless from his long journey. His thick, jet-black hair covered his head. She adored his black eyes locked on hers. Everyone faded into the background as mother and son began to get to know one another. He strained his neck to see his new earthly angel smiling back at him. Everything inside Danyella screamed, *I can't believe I get to do this again someday!*

Danyella felt a love—love like she had never experienced—wrap around her and baby Jonathan as Dr. Jay stitched her up. John, Jacky, and Danyella's mom gathered around her and shared the precious moment of new life. It was by far the most amazing experience of Danyella's life thus far. She knew deep in her heart that it would only get better from that moment on.

CHAPTER 11

LIVING CLOSE TO HEAVEN

Danyella had no trouble getting to sleep that night. Her body and mind were exhausted from the two days of labor. The next morning, when she opened her eyes, she could barely believe that her baby had finally arrived. The previous fifty-five hours seemed like a long, hazy dream. But there he was … cozied up in his little blanket and topped with a cotton hospital hat.

John woke up in the armchair on the other side of the room, stretched, and smiled at his wife. "We have a baby, honey!"

"And the most beautiful baby I might add! Will you bring him to me please?" Danyella asked with childlike anticipation.

Just as John began to pick up their sleeping baby, a nurse walked in. "Good morning!" she said softly. "I'm Monica. I'll be your nurse this morning. How was the first night?"

"He slept right along with us," Danyella said, chuckling. "I think we were all tired from the last two days of work."

"I bet! I'm going to take his vitals and see how he's doing."

Danyella was anxious to hold her baby; but it also felt as if the vitals were taking way longer than normal.

Finally, the nurse looked up. "He's a little below temperature. Nothing to worry about. This is a perfect opportunity for some skin-to-skin time with Mom."

Danyella smiled and held out her arms. Next she quickly unclothed her chest, picked up her baby, and laid him on the surgically scarred area of her breast. Nurse Monica wrapped the two of them in warm blankets.

Danyella felt at home with her baby. It was a beautiful high like she had never experienced before. Their love felt magical. She could have stayed wrapped up with her baby forever, but her stomach didn't agree. After an hour of snuggling, Danyella knew it was time to eat. Nurse Monica came in and made the separation a little easier by needing to take his temperature. Danyella kissed his little cheeks and smelled his neck before reluctantly letting him go. Nurse Monica's face flushed with concern as she read the thermometer. "What is it?" Danyella asked.

"I'm going to call the doctor. Jonathan's temperature seems to have dropped. That's the opposite of what should have happened since he just had skin-to-skin time with you."

Danyella didn't know what to say. John came to her side. "Everything's going to be OK, honey." She grabbed his hand. She felt a blanket of confident energy surrounding her; she knew that her angels were reassuring her that everything was all right.

Dr. Elliot walked in and introduced himself; Danyella was comforted by his calm demeanor. "I'll check out your little man. The nurses tell me that he's been dropping in temperature, which could be dangerous if we don't treat it right away."

He looked at the vital chart and pulled out a thermometer to take Jonathan's temperature. "Hi there, Mister Jonathan. So glad you could join us. Your mom and dad are over the moon to meet you, and it sure is my pleasure too. You seem a little cold, buddy. Let's take care of that, OK?"

Danyella smiled. She was sure her baby was feeling the doctor's positive energy too.

He bundled Jonathan back up and then spoke to Danyella and John. "I don't want to scare you, but he seems to be declining in temperature, which is a concern. His temperature's not critical at the moment, but we don't want to take the chance of it going any farther in that direction. I'll admit him to the NICU and wait on him hand and foot." His smile was soft and serious at the same time. "Any questions?"

"Will we be able to see him?" John asked nervously.

"He can have visitors. We encourage you two to be in there as much as possible. Any hour of the day or night. Just make sure you're healing and taking care of yourself too, Mom."

The new parents both expelled deep breaths and thanked the doctor. Danyella kissed Jonathan before Nurse Monica wheeled him out of the room and down the hall. John kissed Danyella's forehead. Danyella wanted to cry, but she held in her tears, so as not to worry her husband. They embraced, which seemed to melt away her nervousness.

Danyella did exactly as Dr. Elliot had instructed and took care of herself first. She ate a big breakfast and did everything Nurse Monica asked of her before having John help her into the wheelchair to travel to the NICU. She just couldn't wait to see her precious baby again.

As they entered the NICU, a nurse instructed them on the unit's entering and exiting procedures. Danyella saw incubators that held babies, some of which were only the size of large pickles. Danyella scrubbed her hands and forearms at the entrance sink and waited impatiently as John did the same. John pushed Danyella around the aisles of cribs. Danyella felt a big rush of gratitude for this place that took such amazing care of fragile babies and especially hers. When she spotted the warming crib and her baby's sweet headful of hair, her heart rushed with love and her eyes welled up with tears.

She couldn't transfer into the rocking chair to hold her baby fast enough. Cuddling Jonathan was her new favorite pastime, and John's new favorite pastime was watching his wife and baby together. The proud parents spent several hours cooing over how perfect he was and passing him back and forth. It was the most wonderful love they had ever experienced. Time ceased to exist for Danyella and John. The only thing that brought them back to reality was the rumbling in their hungry bellies for dinner.

"I'll get us some food, honey. I'll come grab you when it's in your room," John said.

"Thanks, honey. I think it's almost time for some medication too," Danyella said while adjusting herself in the chair. Danyella held her baby and thought about the entire journey up to that point. She thought about Maya. *What does this mean? Is this you in my arms? Or are you still watching over me?* She felt a new presence with her baby boy, but she wanted to be positive so she asked for a sign.

She caught a glimpse of a green tag that was dangling over Jonathan's incubator crib. She placed him in the crib and grasped the tag. Her eyes filled with tears as she realized that the tag read 22. *You're watching over us, huh, baby girl?* She smiled. She felt goose bumps on her arms. It brought back a vivid memory from several years earlier, one time when she was in a dimly lit room across from a psychic at a palm reading. The woman had closed her eyes and tilted her face toward the ceiling as Danyella shared a few intuitions she was curious about. While doing so, she felt goose bumps. "*Oooh!* I just got goose bumps!"

"You know what that means?" the woman asked with a smile.

"No I don't." Danyella leaned in.

"It means the angels are nodding in agreement or proclaiming truth has been spoken."

Danyella smiled at the distant memory and knew that Maya was proclaiming Danyella's discovery as truth. She was thrilled to finally be a mother, but she took great comfort in knowing that she would continue her spiritual connection with Maya.

Three days of bliss passed before it was time for Danyella to be discharged from the hospital. She would have been thrilled to go home, but Jonathan wasn't ready to be discharged from the NICU. She just didn't feel right going home without him. "I'm not leaving here without my baby," she told John and her nurses.

"We understand your concern. You can stay at our care center across the street. It's for friends and family who are waiting for their family members to heal. We can let you stay free of charge for two nights," Nurse Monica said.

"Thank you so much!" Danyella replied. She wanted to be near her baby no matter the cost. She felt confident that her angels would work behind the scenes to get her baby discharged before her two days were up. *All is well*, she told herself.

As if Nurse Monica had heard Danyella's thought, she said, "All is well," and patted Danyella's leg.

Earthly angels are all around me. Danyella felt stunned at such an amazingly synchronized unfolding of her thoughts turning into reality.

She spent every moment she could in the NICU; she left Jonathan's side only to sleep and eat. The moment she woke up in the morning, she brushed her teeth, got dressed, and rushed across the street to her baby. The mere thought of holding him made her feel more alive than she had ever felt before. Her feet began swelling due to all the extra walking to and from the hospital, but she hushed her worries and focused on getting to see her beautiful baby. She loved nuzzling her nose into his tiny neck. He had that amazing newborn baby smell that she just couldn't get enough of. She inhaled deeply every time she held him.

At the NICU, Danyella waved at the nurses and hurried over as fast as she could to the hand station to clean up. She smiled when she saw her son awake and wiggling around in his crib. Her heart felt so full in the presence of him.

"Good morning, Mom!"

Danyella turned to see a happy NICU nurse she hadn't met before. "Hi! Good morning."

"My name is Svetlana. I'm the morning shift nurse who'll be watching Jonathan today. The night nurse just filled me in on his condition, and I wanted to go over a few things with you."

"Nice to meet you," Danyella said as they shook hands.

"It looks like Jonathan hasn't been peeing, which is a concern. If you change him, please mark on this chart what the result of his diaper was so that we can closely monitor his waste."

"OK. I'll also ask him to pee," Danyella said with a wink. Svetlana giggled. Danyella made light of the situation, but she also knew her baby could hear her and would respond.

She picked up Jonathan, and the world seemed to disappear. "Good morning, handsome! You look more beautiful today than you did yesterday!" Danyella smiled at him and rested his head on her shoulder as she positioned herself in the rocking chair. "Mommy has a favor to ask you. I need you to pee to show the doctors that you're ready to come home with me, OK?" Danyella asked in her sweetest voice. She felt confident that all she needed to do was ask, and it would be done. *All you have to do is ask, and it's given.*

Several snuggles, kisses, and a couple of hours later, Jonathan's tiny mouth widened for the cutest yawn Danyella had ever seen. It naturally made her yawn too, which reminded her how tired she was. She rocked him to sleep and remembered the nurse's firm rule about never falling asleep with the baby in your arms. She rose from the chair and put him in his crib. She looked down at her swollen feet that looked as if they were going to burst. She had been getting up before the sun and staying with her son past midnight. Her love for him had made her temporarily forget about her own needs, including her swollen feet. Sitting down again, she pulled up another chair, propped up her frail feet, and closed her eyes.

John arrived to find Danyella fast asleep in the rocking chair next to Jonathan's incubator crib. He smiled at the sight of both of them sleeping alongside one another.

"Hello. My name is Svetlana, and I'm the nurse on duty today. You're John, right? We love seeing involved parents here. Most parents are extremely emotional and nervous because their babies are so fragile. It's nice to watch parents get as involved as your wife has been. She's making my job much easier."

"Nice to meet you. Thank you. Yes, I'm Jonathan's dad. How's he doing today?"

"He's doing well. We're eagerly waiting for him to pee. It might be a good time to check."

John unwrapped the blankets swaddling Jonathan and removed his oversized diaper. "Success!"

"Wonderful!" Svetlana cheered.

The happy commotion woke Danyella. She smiled at the sight of John taking care of Jonathan. She loved seeing them together.

"Good morning, sunshine!" John said cheerfully.

"Morning, honey," Danyella said while she yawned and stretched.

"Our baby peed, honey!"

That perked Danyella up. She stood up and rushed to her husband's side. "I knew you'd listen to your momma!" she said proudly as she stroked her son's hair. The parents smiled at each other as they cooed over their newest family member. To Danyella, nothing had ever felt better than this.

The blissful feeling that came with the arrival of Jonathan made Danyella's two day stay at the hotel across the street feel like mere hours. Danyella hoped that she could take her baby home the same day she was being discharged, but the nurses and doctors were still concerned. Jonathan had finally urinated and even pooped, but now, he was bleeding a little longer than normal from his circumcision. Danyella didn't know how to ask him to stop bleeding, so she asked her angels to ensure his health and safety while keeping them together. After her request, Danyella felt an aura of unwavering faith that everything was going to be alright.

When Dr. Elliot told her about possibly delaying Jonathan's discharge, she just thanked him for keeping her baby safe. "All in perfect timing," Danyella responded in confidence.

Her positive attitude seemed to stump Dr. Elliot. In all his years of working in the NICU, he had never met a parent with such positivity. Her energy was infectious.

The NICU nurses also began to speak positively about the likelihood that Jonathan would be discharged that afternoon despite the bleeding concern. Checklists for discharge were made and reviewed with the parents. "When we get the good news, he'll be released," she was told.

Dr. Elliot arrived in the NICU for Jonathan's afternoon exam; the staff were full of an unusually upbeat energy. Danyella noticed the doctor's concern when he saw Jonathan's car seat ready for a presumed departure. Danyella just smiled sweetly. "Hello, Doctor. Good afternoon!"

"Good afternoon," he said with a polite nod. "You've brought our department a dose of optimistic cheer that's quite refreshing."

"Thank you!" Danyella blushed at the compliment.

"But it's Mr. Jonathan, here, who's the man of the hour and whose exam will determine if he's ready to go home." Dr. Elliot said in a calm but stern voice.

Nurse Svetlana's expression tightened at the doctor's command. She rushed to his side and began to record the measurements he spoke out loud.

"Very good. Very good," he said as he poked and prodded, causing Jonathan to squirm and wiggle. Danyella grasped John's hand in anticipation of the results.

After a thorough examination and a review of the nurses' notes, Dr. Elliot said, "He's thriving, and his bleeding has seemed to slow down as we had hoped. I'm positive that he'll continue to improve just as well if not better at home, so I'm happy to say he can go home today."

The small group of nurses cheered. John and Danyella beamed as they thanked the doctor. Everyone had a smile, even Dr. Elliot.

Walking out of the hospital with her baby that afternoon, Danyella knew something magical had happened. She was starting to understand how focusing on the outcomes she desired, rather than the outcomes that looked most likely, was extremely powerful. She realized that what she turned her attention to did in fact change her reality. She had read and learned so much about this in all her books about the law of attraction, but experiencing it firsthand was what had really taught her. Her favorite author, Abraham Hicks, was right: "Words don't teach. Life experience does."

CHAPTER 12

MY LITTLE DUCKY

Danyella felt overjoyed being at home with her newborn. Every moment was either new and exciting or sweet and tender. She marveled at how this new way of life had become her new normal. She felt so lucky to be gifted this role called motherhood. She even delighted in the endless number of bottles needing to be cleaned, the never-ending loads of baby laundry, and the midnight feedings. Her new role was exhausting but extremely gratifying. The loss of her pregnancy with Maya and the long wait she had endured, trying to conceive Jonathan, had given her a unique focus that encouraged her to savor every minute. She regarded him as her greatest blessing.

One morning, Danyella was joyfully deciding what Jonathan should wear when she remembered the ducky footy pajamas. She squealed with delight at the thought of finally filling the pj's with her baby. She rushed to her overstuffed closet and let her hand run along all her clothing till it settled on the sweet, soft, cottony fabric of the baby pajamas. Pulling them out, she examined the fabric as if she were receiving the gift for the first time. They were the cutest baby pajamas she had ever seen. Alongside her excitement came the memories of her pain and sorrow. Recounting the moments of anguish instantly made her focus on the amount of time between those moments and the current blissful one she was experiencing. It hadn't been that long ago that she had been drowning in despair, but here she was, sitting with her desire right in front of her and in complete, rapturous joy. *That didn't take as long as I had dreaded! You were right, Maya.*

Jonathan's bright black eyes twinkled at her as she undressed him; he squirmed with the touch of the open air on his skin. She folded his legs and arms into the fabric, quickly buttoned up the front, and smiled at him with delight. "Here I am with the cutest baby in the world wearing the cutest pajamas in the world!" she said, in a tone of voice she used only for him. *I wish I could go back and tell my past self that it all will work out.*

You can! she heard distinctly.

What? How? Danyella knew Maya would guide her through her thoughts, so she began a conversation about what she already understood. *I know that time isn't necessarily linear as we like to think here on earth.* Goose bumps … She knew the goose bumps were a sign that Maya was saying yes. *It's more fluid than we think it is. So all I need to do is think about a time when the old me was in distress and tell myself how amazing the future is so that the past me can feel it too!* More goose bumps spread throughout her body. She looked at her wide-eyed baby staring at her. "Well, Mr. Ducky! Every time you get goose bumps, the angels are trying to let you know you're speaking truth."

His black, fuzzy hair and caramel skin seemed to pair perfectly with the soft white and yellow fabric of the prized pajamas. She had never seen anything so sweet. It was like they were made just for him.

Danyella was determined to give her new theory a try. Part of her felt silly, but she also felt a reassurance in Maya's guidance. She reminded herself that it couldn't hurt to try, and at the least, it would feel great to focus on all her current positive feelings.

She sat in her favorite meditation spot in the living room, holding sleepy Jonathan in her arms. She focused on her breathing and began to remember those dreaded moments from the past. Her old fear filled her energy like a black cloud. It felt more depressing than she remembered. It felt dark, lonely, and hopeless, which instantly made Danyella's throat tighten and her eyes well with tears. Consciously redirecting her thoughts, she focused on the physical sensation of Jonathan in her arms. Instantly, she felt a wave of clarity rise within her about all things being well. The good feeling rushed through her body, clearing out the low vibration of her sadness.

She paused not knowing what to do next. She thought of how Maya always spoke to her softly whenever she needed encouragement, so she began to speak to her past self. *In a very short time, those beautiful pajamas will be filled by the most gorgeous baby you will have ever seen. You'll laugh with joy to see how cute the pajamas look on your baby. You'll feel complete, and you'll have a sense of beauty, joy, and rightness when you see your baby in these pajamas. I promise you this and much more.* With tears running down her cheeks, she pulled Jonathan up close to her face for a kiss. "Isn't that right, Mr. Ducky?" Jonathan yawned and stretched.

From that day on, Danyella thought of Jonathan any time she saw a yellow ducky. It became his symbol, and she gravitated to anything that bore it; it would remind her of him even when they were apart. She enjoyed the symbol that represented her firstborn child.

That evening while Danyella was brushing her teeth, she glanced at the clock at exactly twenty-two minutes after the hour. She felt Maya's energy. *Hi, baby girl! I discovered something beautiful today! I found a symbol for your brother, a yellow duckling, and it reminds me of him every time I see one. What symbol should we give you?*

Just as she asked the question, Jonathan's bath soap bottle caught her eye. She followed her intuition and picked up the bottle; a bumblebee was in the middle of the label's design. *A bumblebee! That's your symbol, isn't it, baby girl?* Danyella asked with joy; she felt the rightness of her discovery and Maya's joyful energy all around her.

"What did you say, honey?" John called out from the other room.

Danyella blushed. "Nothing, honey!"

John came from around the corner with an interested grin. "What are you so giddy about?" John asked her playfully.

Danyella felt conflicted; she wanted to share the amazing relationship she had found with their daughter, but she thought, *What would he think of me if I told him I've been talking to the spirit of our dead baby?* "I was just remembering something funny Jacky said the other day."

"It must have been funny considering how much you're glowing!"

Danyella blushed at the thought that she was glowing.

The following week, Danyella began to see bees everywhere—photos of them, live bees on flowers, on TV commercials, on products in the store … She couldn't believe how many daily encounters she was having with bees; she felt a rush of excitement and love every time she saw one. It was Maya's new way of saying hello and loving her mother. Danyella savored her daughter's attention and affection. It was the most adoring love Danyella had ever felt from another person.

CHAPTER 13

AUNT SAMANTHA

Jonathan seemed to be growing daily; it wasn't long before Danyella realized that his first birthday was quickly approaching. Now, she finally understood why her mother always said that time was speeding by too quickly when she was young. *Time flies when you're having fun!* She giggled as she hugged her growing baby.

That summer, Aunt Samantha and Uncle Leonard flew out to meet the baby before his first birthday. Danyella was excited to see them. Their visits were few and far between because Florida seemed worlds apart from the Pacific Northwest. She just loved being around her aunt. She looked up to her in so many ways, and it showed in their many common interests.

At the airport, Danyella spotted them waiting for their luggage. Aunt Samantha was wearing a stylish sundress covered with bright summer flowers, a big sun hat, and Audrey Hepburn–influenced sunglasses. Uncle Leonard looked plain next to her in his tan shirt and khaki pants, but Danyella always remembered him saying, "I like being the wallflower next to this stunning dahlia."

Danyella stood at a distance and waited a bit before greeting them because she liked watching them interact. They were picking on each other in a very amusing and endearing way. Danyella giggled softly and smiled at their loving interaction. Aunt Samantha always knew when Danyella was nearby even if she couldn't be seen; it was one of her many gifts. She let Danyella believe that she wasn't aware she was watching them from afar and continued to pick on Uncle Leonard a little harder for entertainment.

Finally, Danyella waved at her loved ones from across several baggage claim stations. Aunt Samantha's face lit up like a Christmas tree. "Come on, Lenny! There she is!" Aunt Samantha shouted as she grabbed her luggage and started marching right toward Jonathan, who was on Danyella's hip.

"*Oooohhh!* He's perfect!" Aunt Samantha clasped her hands in front of her chest as if in prayer. Danyella smiled and leaned in for a hug; she caught the aroma of her aunt's essential oils—lavender and cedar wood. Danyella loved those smells.

Uncle Lenny hugged Danyella from the side and kissed her forehead. "How are you, my dear?"

"I'm in baby heaven … Every day!"

"We couldn't be happier for you, dear. Hand over that little man!" Aunt Samantha said.

"More like hand over that little sumo wrestler," Uncle Leonard joked. "What are you feeding him?" Uncle Leonard let Jonathan grab his finger. They laughed and smiled ear to ear.

As they drove to Danyella's mom's house, their conversation had no end—and no awkward pauses. The women had an endless stream of exciting topics to report to one another; they barely took breaths between sentences—one exciting conversation after another; Uncle Leonard wasn't able to get a word in edgewise as the women constantly completed each other's sentences.

After many different subjects, tons of laughter, and Uncle Leonard finally tuning himself out of their conversations, they pulled into Danyella's mom's driveway and saw her waiting on the porch. She rushed to the car and helped her guests with their bags. "Welcome back!" she said as she kissed Aunt Samantha on the cheek and hugged Uncle Leonard.

"Thank you, sis!" Aunt Samantha said as they headed toward the house. Danyella waved goodbye from the car as she pulled out of the driveway to go to a doctor's appointment. She wished she was staying at her mother's house; her mom most likely had a large pitcher of tea and a tray of pimento cheese and crackers waiting for them on the back deck. Her delightful daydreaming about being with her family almost made her miss the turn for her doctor's office building.

Just as she arrived in the waiting room, a woman in pink scrubs, with short mocha hair and a toothy smile walked in and announced Danyella's name. *Perfect timing!* Danyella steered the stroller with sleeping Jonathan down the narrow hallway after the nurse.

"Dr. Lynn will be right with you," the nurse said, pointing to an exam room to her right.

Dr. Lynn, her doctor, was the only doctor Danyella knew who wore a full face of makeup to work; she loved her uniqueness. She always looked like she was going someplace fancy after work. Dr. Lynn scurried into the room in a hurry. Danyella was reading a magazine while sitting on the crinkly paper on the exam table. "Hi, Danyella! How are you?" Dr. Lynn said as she peeked up from her clipboard of notes.

"Great! Timed this appointment so that it landed in the middle of his nap time," Danyella said all proud as she pointed to Jonathan with a smile.

"That's talent!" Dr. Lynn replied as she cleaned her hands with hand sanitizer. "I received your uterus ultrasound images. It looks like you do have a uterus abnormality." Danyella's smile vanished. Seriousness filled the room. "It's nothing to stress over. You have what we call an arcuate uterus. Essentially, there's a little dip at the top of the uterus. Some people refer to this as a heart-shaped uterus. But yours is very minor. And the good news is that since you went full term with Jonathan, it's possible for you to conceive and carry again."

"Does that explain why my birth went the way it did, Doctor?"

"Yes and no. There's no way to say for sure that the shape of your uterus caused so many complications, but it definitely could be a major factor. Going into your next pregnancy, you'll have much more information and awareness that can help you and your practitioner make earlier decisions on your birth plan," Dr. Lynn said optimistically. Danyella liked her positive attitude especially on this subject. "I'll send you home with more information about your diagnosis. This is nothing to worry about, just something to be informed about and how it might affect you and your pregnancies," Dr. Lynn said while typing her notes into the computer. She looked at Danyelle, touched her patient's elbow for comfort, and smiled. "Thanks for letting me be a part of your heart-filled journey," Dr. Lynn said endearingly.

Danyella blushed and smiled kindly at Dr. Lynn's thoughtfulness.

She felt a mix of emotions on her drive back to her mom's house. She felt relieved about finally having an answer, but it also seemed to cast a shadow of fear. Pregnancy hadn't come so easily the first or the second time. *Was that all due to my abnormal womb? Was I somehow at fault?* Despite her normal emphasis on positive thinking, she felt raw emotion overpowering her good-feeling beliefs. She needed some relief from her mind's battle; she wanted to come back to it after she was ready to focus on her desirable outcome.

She always felt good thinking about Jonathan, a great distraction. *He's perfectly unperfected in the right amount, which makes him even more perfect.* Danyella giggled at the anomaly. *He's everything I hoped for and more. The universe must have created him out of my dreams and desires. He's more than I dreamed possible. His perfection reminds me that everything always works out.* And just like that, her affirmations shifted her energy in the direction she wanted. Thinking of him was a surefire way for her to feel good.

She felt an ecstatic rush of gratitude for her wonderful life and her sleeping baby. She almost floated out of her car and into her mother's house with Jonathan, who was trying to wake from his afternoon nap. She walked into the house and smelled her mom's enchiladas baking in the oven. Danyella noticed that the living room with powder-blue walls and two cream couches facing each other was extra tidy today. Her attention quickly sprang to the new beach-themed throw pillows that that her mom must have purchased in honor of her guests, which complemented the seashells that decorated the room.

She carried Jonathan down the hallway toward the back of the house and found her family members on the deck, enjoying iced tea and pimento cheese and crackers, just like she had suspected. She knew her mom very well. At the sight of Danyella, Uncle Leonard jumped up to get first dibs on holding his great-nephew.

"What did the doctor say?" Danyella's mom asked brightly.

"I have an arcuate uterus. That means it's shaped like a heart at the top."

"That's why you walked through the door full of *love*?" Aunt Samantha asked with a wink.

Danyella giggled. "Oh, my good mood? I'd just been reminding myself of all that's going so well in my world. I guess you could tell."

"I'm sure the whole neighborhood could feel you, dear. You're happier than a clam in salt water."

Danyella always wore her feelings on her sleeve; when she was on a high, everyone felt it.

"So when do we get to meet that granddaughter of mine?" Danyella's mother asked.

"In perfect timing," Danyella said sweetly with a wink.

Enjoying her mother's enchilada dinner and the company of her loved ones, Danyella wondered exactly why the day had felt so good. Maybe it was because things were more complete with her aunt and uncle there; it always felt like something was missing when they were gone. Danyella usually spent every waking hour at her mom's house during their visits so she could soak in those wonderful memories of them all being together. Danyella and her aunt always had interesting conversations particularly when her aunt predicted the future. She was what some people called psychic. Family and friends always jumped at the chance to hear what she thought their futures might hold.

With Jonathan peacefully snuggling in her arms, Aunt Samantha told Danyella what she saw in her eyes. "You've been waiting impatiently for your daughter, my dear." That got Danyella's attention; she smiled bashfully and nodded. "It's coming, darling. She's waiting for the right time."

"I'm trying to be patient, but I'm just so excited about meeting her here on earth."

"You know that one is a girl?" her aunt asked.

"Absolutely!" But then Danyella was puzzled. "Did you say that one is a girl?"

"Yes, there are two girls with you. One of them is the baby you speak of often from your miscarriage, and the other one is right along with her," Aunt Samantha said with sureness. That perked up Danyella even more. "That's probably why you've been seeing so many signs of twins. I think they might be coming together," Aunt Samantha said with an enchanting smile.

Danyella's eyes welled up with happy tears. "That would make so much sense!"

"Come here, dear." Aunt Samantha waved Danyella over. Danyella sat, and her aunt put her hand on her belly and looked off into the distance. Danyella held her breath with anticipation of what she would predict. Her aunt looked puzzled. "I see the number two twice."

"You mean twenty-two?"

"Oh yes, you're right. Not sure what month twenty-two would be. Maybe the baby will arrive on the twenty-second," Aunt Samantha said with wink.

"Twenty-two is the number my baby uses to communicate with me!" Danyella said as she beamed.

"Everything will happen in good timing, sweet girl," Aunt Samantha said as they hugged in celebration.

That evening as Danyella drove home with Jonathan asleep in the back seat, her mind ran wild. She was still in shock about there being two girls. It was definitely something she would have to get used to. *So there are two of you? If one of you is Maya, who's the other?* A name clear as day floated to her mind—*Sofia*. Danyella smiled and felt a rush of joy flood her body. *That is so wonderful! I get my Sofia after all!*

For the first time in a long time, Danyella felt her true worth; she felt loved and adored and in the center of pure, positive energy. She decided to state out loud a list of positive aspects. "I'm thankful for my girls!" The words *my girls* resonated in her heart and mind; they sounded even more beautiful out loud. "I'm thankful for all the wonderful circumstances that led me to where I am today. I'm thankful for my Aunt Samantha being the portal through which this sweet information arrived. I'm thankful for my beautiful son, who came first to bring reality to my lifelong desire of being a mommy! He's the best thing I could've asked for."

When John saw Danyella's car arrive, he walked outside to help her inside the house. Danyella wanted to add John to her list of positive aspects, but she was too shy to say it out loud in front of him. Instead, she felt the joy of it while she thought about her gratitude for him in her mind. When he kissed her, he felt her bliss and returned a smile. He stared into Danyella's sea-blue eyes, and they nodded as if agreeing with one another about the happiness of the moment. They didn't need words. Their magnetic love in the air was enough.

CHAPTER 14

SOFIA

That night as Danyella got ready for bed, her eyes fell on the bumblebee logo on Jonathan's lotion bottle; she felt Maya saying hello. Danyella wondered if Sofia would pick something to remind her of her presence too. *Your brother's symbol is a ducky, and Maya's is a bumblebee. What's your symbol, Sofia?* When no answer floated into her mind, she thought, *I see … You want Momma to discover it in a fun way. Game on, girl! I'll be keeping my eye out for it.* But she knew it would appear in its own time.

Danyella spent many moments that week conversing with her daughters. It was fun to pick up on the differences in each of their energies. Maya had a bold, lively personality, a lot like Danyella's, while Sofia's energy was as subtle as John's. Danyella loved getting to know them. Without physical bodies or earthly personalities, getting to know her daughters flowed more easily. Since their energy was so pure, the depths of who they were shone brightly, allowing Danyella to get to know them more quickly than anyone she had met on earth.

119

"Kiki, I'm so lucky! I know that most people fall in love with the thought of their children, but here I am having full-on relationships before they even arrive! That blows my mind!"

Kiki was fanning her sun-kissed skin with her menu; they were at their favorite Italian restaurant for lunch one Saturday. Kiki smiled and nodded. "I totally understand how you feel about your girls. My relationship with my twin boys was similar. I didn't talk to them like you are with yours, but I feel their love. I know they're with me."

"I love that! You never told me very much about your twin boys, but I believe that babies who don't make it here on earth usually become guides for their mommas."

"I never thought about it that way before, but yes, that makes sense. I feel that my boys have guided me many times and still come around for big events. It's so hard to explain, but I just always know they're there. It's like I can feel them."

Danyella felt so touched that Kiki was sharing something so personal. "If anyone understands what you mean, it would be me. I feel crazy for even saying out loud that I can hear my girls in my thoughts. It's tough to explain. I believe that we all have the ability to communicate with our loved ones on the other side. I just hear more than most because I've practiced being open to it. Once you start, it's like exercising a muscle to strengthen it. You get better and better at it."

"Yes! I feel the same way about trusting my intuition. The more I listen to it, the clearer it becomes."

Danyella smiled at the thought of being completely understood by her friend. She loved that she could tell Kiki anything and that even if Kiki didn't fully understand, she would try to learn. It was an openness Danyella often wished she shared with John, but sitting next to her open-minded friend, she felt that, eventually, anything was possible.

There wasn't a day that Danyella's girls weren't on her mind or showing up in her experience somewhere. The number twenty-two was even starting to show up around her family members. Most of Danyella's family and friends weren't aware why they felt compelled to bring up their stories about this number, but she knew. She wasn't surprised anymore when someone would mention twenty-two several times within a conversation. She knew it was her daughters' way of saying they were with her loved ones too.

The weekend Jonathan turned nine months old, Danyella woke to a warm summer breeze, along with the scent of flowers flowing in from her open bedroom window. *What a lovely way to wake up!* The sunlight and the smell of the flowers was a sign that she had slept in; John and Jonathan were already up.

She slipped out of bed and tiptoed to see what fun her boys were up to. She found them in the dining room with expressions of confusion as John attempted to mix Jonathan's oatmeal with fruit the way Danyella normally did. She peered in for a moment at the unique moment of fatherhood John was facing before walking to her husband's side and wrapping her arms around his shoulder. "Good job, Daddy! It's starting to look … uh … delicious."

John scoffed. "You're being kind! I'm not sure I'm doing this right."

"You've seen me do it a thousand times," Danyella chuckled, and John laughed as he encouraged happy Jonathan to take a bite.

Danyella's phone rang. The screen showed it was Jacky. "Hi, Jacky!" Danyella said as she trailed off into the living room. She returned to the kitchen a minute or two later wearing a big smile.

"Jacky and the kids have invited us over for rock painting and lunch in their backyard!"

"Got some errands to run. You and Johnathan should go, and I'll meet you there later."

"Sounds perfect, honey," Danyella said, bouncing down the hallway to get ready for her day.

Arriving at her sister's house, she heard her niece and nephew laughing in the backyard. She went around the side of the house and saw them cheerfully painting stones and listening to their favorite summer tunes. Mackenzie looked up from her paint brush and squealed. "Hi, Aunt Danyella!"

Without hesitation, they both put down their paintbrushes and ran to Danyella's side to show off their creations while shouting competitively for her attention. Jonathan giggled at their excitement while perched on Danyella's hip.

"One at a time, kids! Mackenzie, why don't you let your little brother go first?" Danyella said with a wink. Mackenzie reluctantly nodded and looked up at Danyella with her adorable, wide-open hazel eyes. Danyella cherished the sweet relationship she had with her adoring niece.

Isaac held up his painted rock and waited for his aunt to identify what it was.

"That's the best soccer ball rock I've ever seen!" Danyella cooed.

"It's not just any soccer ball, Aunt Danyella! It's a robot soccer ball that can fly around the world in less than twenty-two minutes!"

"Twenty-two minutes, huh? That's superfast!" Danyella gushed. Danyella had gotten good at holding in her reactions when Maya made her presence known; she smiled and felt her heart fill with love. "What did you make, Mackenzie?" Mackenzie pulled a rock from behind her back, and Danyella's heart sang at the sight of a yellow-and-black-striped bumblebee.

"It's a love bug!" Mackenzie said with pride.

"You're such a great artist, Mackenzie!"

"It's not just a bumblebee, Aunt Danyella!"

"Let me guess … It's a robot bumblebee that can fly around the world in under twenty-two minutes?" Danyella asked, giggling.

"No! It's a bee, but it's also a ladybug," Mackenzie said turning the rock over and showing her aunt the ladybug she had painted on the other side.

Danyella realized that Sofia was showing her the symbol she had chosen for herself. "That's so beautiful, Mackenzie!" She loved that her daughters had sent a message through her sweet niece.

"Where's John?" Jacky asked as she walked up to Danyella.

"He's running a few errands. He'll be here shortly."

"At least you brought my favorite little Jonathan!" Jacky said, taking Jonathan from her sister.

Sitting at the picnic table full of paints and brushes, Danyella felt a childlike urge to create a butterfly on one of the rocks. Butterflies were one of her favorite animals; they reminded her of her angels watching over her. She scanned the colors and settled on a pale yellow for her creation. As her brush began to twist and twirl over the rock, Danyella felt an old joy for painting that she had missed. There was definitely something special about being with her niece and nephew, who were full of free-spirited energy. It inspired her to feel freer and more childlike when she was with them. It was a good feeling.

After the rocks were painted and almost dry, John arrived. "Perfect timing, honey!" Danyella said, giving him a kiss hello. Jonathan's eyes lit up at the sight of his daddy. "You ready for a walk around the neighborhood to hide our painted rocks, honey?"

"Sounds wonderful! The wind's starting to pick up, and I forgot a coat. Jacky, does Ben have one I could borrow?"

"I just brought one of his coats in from the garage. He took it camping a few weeks ago and forgot to unpack it, but don't worry— it's clean."

As Jacky led John into the house to retrieve the coat, Danyella and the kids loaded the colorful rocks into the children's wagon. Jonathan snuggled right in on the other end for a ride around the neighborhood. Danyella and Mackenzie were admiring how cute he looked in the wagon when they heard Jacky's thrilling scream. Danyella quickly grabbed Jonathan, and they all ran to the back door of the house. They saw John and Jacky huddled around the coat on the mud room floor. The inside of the coat was covered in a bright-red color. Jacky calmed the commotion by raising her hand in the air as if to say all was well.

"It's the oddest thing!" she said. "This coat that Ben took camping must have been the birthplace for thousands of ladybugs!" Jacky said, as Danyella's heart skipped a happy beat.

"Ladybugs! I wanna see!" Isaac screamed as he pushed his way toward the coat on the floor. In his excitement, he bumped the coat with his foot. The air was suddenly flooded with thousands of baby ladybugs trying to fly. They swished and whirled around the bewildered onlookers. The air was so thick with baby ladybugs that they had to close their mouths not to inhale them. Danyella smiled and Mackenzie giggled as the beautiful bugs danced all around. "How magical!" Jacky shouted.

Magical indeed! Danyella thought, feeling overwhelmed by her daughter's love.

CHAPTER 15

EVERYTHING IN
PERFECT TIMING

Fall—Danyella's favorite season—was fast approaching as the last days of August arrived. She wanted to go to the mall to buy her growing boy some new outfits. She was looking forward to spending some alone time with him and perhaps a coffee and a cinnamon pretzel that only the mall seemed to offer.

Her good mood prior to arriving at the mall seemed to set a string of good-feeling things in motion. Hearing one of her favorite songs on the radio inspired her to blare the music as she drove. The loud, upbeat song encouraged her to sing along. Danyella moved with the motion of the beat as she felt a strong sense of joy. When she arrived at the mall, she easily found what she wanted to buy for Jonathan in the right sizes and all on discount.

"Did you find everything you needed?" the young sales clerk asked.

"Yes, I found more than enough!" Danyella said showing her the stack of clothes in her arms.

"Good! I'm glad you returned in time for the shirt you placed on hold. I was just about to put it back on the shelf."

"Pardon me?" Danyella asked in confusion.

"This shirt," she said holding up a little boy's T-shirt. "I was about to put it back on the rack, but then you showed up. Perfect timing!"

Danyella read the words printed on the shirt: "Promoted to Big Brother!" It was a few sizes too large for Jonathan, but she felt a strange urge to claim ownership. "This wasn't my hold, but I'll buy it!"

"Oh, well, it seems like it was meant for you then." The clerk rang up Danyella's purchases, including the T-shirt.

Danyella smiled as she pondered the serendipitous event and waited patiently for her total. Her intuition picked up on just how special this sign of the future was. She felt loved and proud of her ability to trust the universe and its signs.

Reaching home, she took a closer look at the T-shirt, a size 3-T; that made her laugh. "I guess you won't be getting your promotion to big brother for a little longer unless you plan on doubling in size overnight, my love," she told Jonathan, who giggled at his mom's laughter. "It'll fit you in perfect timing."

The shirt was a sign of a longer journey than she wanted to wait for Maya to arrive. She felt a sting of impatience settle into her energy. She thought about how John had expressed his concerns with having a second child so soon. She knew that trying to explain to

John why she purchased the shirt would come with some difficulty, so she tucked it away in the bottom of her dresser, where it would remain her and Jonathan's little secret.

Despite how long Danyella thought it would take for Jonathan to grow into the shirt, she noted that he was indeed growing and fast. Along with his growth came an explosion of what he needed including a growing toy collection. Danyella and John were feeling cramped in their apartment that used to fit the two of them so well, so she stared looking for a house to rent. She was in no rush; she wanted to find the perfect next place for the three of them. She dreamed of a buying a place of their own, but they weren't in the financial position to do that; they had debts to pay down before that could happen, so the next best thing was a rental house with a yard.

Only a few weeks into her exciting journey, she stumbled upon the perfect two-bedroom house in the perfect neighborhood with the perfect little yard. Danyella giggled with delight as she flipped through the pictures of the quaint place online. After looking at the photos, she had visions of Jonathan running around the spacious living room, the three of them playing in the backyard, and baking up a storm in the luxurious kitchen. These visions felt so good that as soon as John walked in the door after work that evening, she announced, "Honey, we're moving!"

"You found us a new place?" John asked with a weary smile.

"Yes, a little rental in the perfect part of town!" Danyella squealed while waving him over to join her at the computer screen. He made a detour to the kitchen to drop his lunch pail off before making his way over to Danyella; he liked making her wait even just a few extra seconds because he knew how impatient she was.

Danyella clicked through the photos while John nodded and smiled. Danyella knew her husband well; his subtle expression of joy ran deeper. "It's perfect for us, honey!"

"It does look sorta perfect," John agreed almost in disbelief.

"*And* ..." Danyella continued dramatically, "it's well within our budget! Can you believe it? It couldn't be any more perfect!"

She didn't know it, but John was already sold. Her desire for a bigger place had rubbed off on him over the last few weeks. "Let's not waste any time, honey. How do we apply?"

Danyella was thrilled with his enthusiasm. "I thought you might feel that way, so I already filled out the application. I'll send it off since we agree. I'm so excited, honey! I have such a great feeling about this!"

After submitting the rental application, the landlord seemed to take a while to respond. Danyella didn't mind; instead, she spent the time dreaming about moving in and where all their furniture would go, and she even started thinking about what recipes she'd bake in the large kitchen. She assumed that the place was theirs, and she even packed up some things they didn't use frequently.

That afternoon, her phone rang. She didn't recognize the number. "This could be about the house!" she told Jonathan, her only audience. "Hello?" she asked in her most charming voice.

A soft-spoken woman answered, "Hi, Danyella?"

"Yes, this is Danyella," she said trying not to sound too overjoyed.

"Hello, Danyella. My name's Mary. I'm calling about your application for the rental on Seventy-Eighth Street."

"Yes, I was looking forward to your call."

"I wanted to find out if you're still interested in the place. We have one applicant ahead of you, but we've had several ahead of them not work out, so we're going down the list."

"Yes! My husband and I are very interested in the house. It would fit our little family perfectly," Danyella replied cheerfully.

"Great! I'll give you a call in a few days if you're the applicants we decide to go with. We enjoyed reading your lovely letter about your little family with your application."

"Oh good! I always like to give my landlords a little more heartfelt info than an application can provide. Thank you!" Danyella said as she walked in circles in her living room. Ending the phone call, she did a little jump. "It's ours, little baby! I just know it!"

The week went by quickly. Waiting for the landlord's decision was surprisingly easy for Danyella and John. They were so satisfied with their decision to move that it was almost as if they didn't need the real manifestation to enjoy it. Danyella already felt that they were there. That was something new for her. She had previously always needed her desires to be in a physical form before she could enjoy them, but she was getting the same level of enjoyment from just simply thinking about the house. It was an amazing feeling. Everything she desired was ultimately in pursuit of feeling good. This new discovery felt life-changing. She felt that she had just uncovered the quickest way to happiness and that she had spent a large part of her life looking at things in a backward way. Things no longer had to be in her hands before she could enjoy the energy of them. She was starting to realize that her mind was a very powerful thing.

CHAPTER 16

TWENTY-TWO'S MESSAGE

Danyella's and John's excitement about the rental came with a new type of energy that was infectious. And fun started showing up everywhere. They were going to bed with long lists of things they were grateful for and waking up excited to see what the day would bring. Life was good.

Danyella was enjoying all the beautiful signs she was receiving from the universe including the number twenty-two, which was showing up everywhere and constantly reminding her that Maya was there saying hello.

One afternoon right at 3:22, her phone rang. She grinned. *I don't know that number, but you're telling me it's something good, huh, little girl?*

"Hello, Danyella?"

"Yes?" Danyella tried to remain calm; she recognized the woman's voice.

"Hi. This is Mary for the rental house on Seventy-Eighth. I wanted to let you know that we've selected another applicant for the house, but we are so thankful for your application. I wanted to call you personally to give you the news just in case you were waiting on us."

Danyella was shocked. She went pale. It felt like it took minutes for her brain to catch up. "Oh all right. No problem. Thank you for calling, Mary. I appreciate it."

The stunning call ended quickly, and Danyella felt the numbness of disappointment creep in. She felt as if someone had punched her in the stomach. But a thought struck her. *Just have faith that all will work out better than planned.* Her intuition calmed her. She took a deep breath and picked up Jonathan. "It's gonna be OK, baby boy. Something better is on its way." Hugging him always filled her with faith that everything did work out. Her baby boy was living proof of that.

When John came home from work that evening, Danyella was sluggishly moving around the kitchen as she cooked. Despite her prior pep talk with herself, she felt the strong sting of disappointment.

"Hi, honey!" John said as he hung up his coat.

"Hi, babe," Danyella responded without looking up from chopping onions.

"Something the matter? Or are the onions just bringing you down?" John joked as he kneeled and opened his arms to embrace Jonathan.

She watched her loving husband and son hugging and smiling broadly. *There's nothing more beautiful than a baby and their parents in love with one another.* "I have some bad news, John."

"Bad news? Nothing could be too terrible considering I have you two to come home to!"

"We didn't get the rental. They picked someone else. I guess we'll be calling this our home for a little while longer."

"So what does my beautiful wife always say when something doesn't work out as planned?"

"That everything happens for a reason and that the universe has bigger plans for us," Danyella said in a reluctant tone.

"Exactly!" he said while pulling her in for a hug.

His hugs always made her worries melt away. She knew he was correct; she much preferred giving rather than receiving such advice from someone who didn't believe in it all the way, but she felt his love in his effort to cheer her up.

"Oh, I almost forgot!" John said. "One of my coworkers' daughters was selling books for a fundraiser today. Nothing interested me, but I found this book for you." He pulled a card-sized book out of his pocket. "It looked like something you'd love, so I bought it."

Danyella took the book from him; it had a picture of several angels on the cover. *"Angel Numbers?"* She felt goose bumps rise on her forearms.

"You love numbers and angels, so I thought it might be something you'd be interested in. It's some sort of dictionary for numbers or something …"

John's voice faded into the background as she flipped through the pages; she gathered that it seemed to decode a language based on numbers. She remembered how Maya had primarily used numbers in the early days of their relationship and how their communication became more dynamic until they were able to hold conversations based purely on energy exchange and thought. But numbers were still a sign of love and comfort in their communication. Danyella didn't fully understand what they meant, but this book felt like a bridge. The pages were filled with explanations for zero to 999.

She scanned the weathered pages feverishly for the number twenty-two that Maya had shown her so many times. She felt her whole body radiate with joy as she read, "Twenty-two—everything's working out better than planned. Have faith that heaven is working behind the scenes on every detail to bring you a spectacular outcome." This message was a warm hug, something she felt when she was happy but often forgot when she was upset. It was a joyful reminder that all is always well.

The rest of the evening, she focused on out what she was grateful for in their apartment; counting her blessings always made her feel better. This was a good opportunity to exercise her new belief that everything always worked out as it was supposed to, even if it didn't feel like it at first. She suddenly felt Maya's presence; it felt like Maya was cheering her on. A warm feeling flooded Danyella; she knew she was focusing in the right direction.

The next morning, Danyella lay in bed waiting to feel her normal Saturday-morning excitement, but her thoughts were anything but enthusiastic. She stared at the ceiling as thoughts circled in her mind like a Ferris wheel making frequent stops at each unstimulating idea to unload its bland contents into her head. It had been some time since she had felt this way. She had focused on the rental house for weeks; that had made her temporarily forget what it was like to wake up in such a disengaged mood.

The sight of Jonathan stretching his arms and legs and arching his belly on the other side of the bed broke her trance. She scrunched her eyes and wiped her face clean of any tension before saying, "Good morning, my love!" The words *my love* brought her an inch closer to her truth about her day. It felt like relief. "Did you sleep well? I'm sure you did! Let's go find Daddy and see what we'll do today!"

John was on the couch drinking coffee and looking at something on his cell phone. Danyella smiled and anticipated his gaze meeting hers shortly, but he was fixated on his phone. "What's so interesting?" she asked as she plopped on the couch with Jonathan in her arms.

"My friend posted about an open house in the area. It's a unique place."

"A house for sale?"

"Yep. I know we weren't thinking about buying, but since we don't have any plans, maybe we should check this place out just for fun at least."

A house for sale? We aren't financially ready to buy. We have way too much debt, and who knows what our credit looks like right now.

John broke her string of negative thoughts. "It's on Twenty-Second Avenue, your favorite number!"

Danyella's face lit up like a kid's on Christmas morning. "Really?" She knew Maya was nudging her in the right direction. "I guess we're going to see a house today!" Danyella told Jonathan in an animated voice causing him to clap and giggle.

On their way to the house, she felt her old feeling of positive expectations set in, much different from her early morning gloom.

She felt much more connected to who she truly was. When John turned onto Twenty-Second Avenue, she peered out at the neighborhood they were embarking on. The houses were well kept with large manicured yards. It wasn't a new neighborhood, but she preferred older houses to newer ones because she felt they had more personality.

"There it is," John said pointing to a house on the corner with a for sale sign. They pulled over and gazed at an alluring front yard of spring flowers. "Look at that garage door!" John said excitedly as they got out of the car and walked up the freshly cemented driveway.

"I don't think I've ever seen one like it," Danyella said. The garage door was paneled with light-green hazed glass that dramatically highlighted the front of the house. It reminded her of the homes she walked past on her way to and from grade school. She had often dreamed of what it would be like to live in such grand houses.

Jonathan toddled his way up the walkway to the entry gate. He giggled as he saw his parents rushing to him and quickened his pace with a devious grin. The gate was open enough that he was able to get through it. Danyella quickly followed through the gate to find a motionless Jonathan mesmerized by the goldfish pond that flowed beneath a footbridge leading to the front door. "Fishy!" he said joyfully while pointing at the pond.

"Oh my goodness! How ...?" Danyella gasped. The sound of trickling water echoed off the enclosed entryway's walls.

"This place is unique!" John said as they looked at the pond.

"Welcome!" someone in the house said through the open front door. Danyella picked up Jonathan and walked in toward a middle-aged, bearded man in a pressed blue shirt and tan slacks. "Hi! My name is Ron. I'm the agent selling this beautiful house. What do you think so far?" he asked and offered her his hand; Danyella always felt that she could tell a lot from a handshake, and Ron's was full of enthusiasm.

"Hi! I'm Danyella, and this is John, and this is Jonathan." She nodded to husband and child.

"This house is unique!" John said as he shook Ron's hand.

"Isn't it? That pond and those fish in the entryway are tranquil. So's the backyard. Take a look around. I'll be here for any questions," Ron said with a smile.

Excited to see the rest of the house, Danyella smiled and forgot to thank Ron as she normally would have. John nodded and followed her while scoping out the view of the backyard through the dining room windows. Strolling through the bedrooms that were double the size of their rooms at the apartment, Danyella began to imagine how she would paint the place and where their furniture would go. Her imagination quickly forgot about the disappointment of the rental house.

"We don't need that rental house anyway!" Danyella said once they were back in the car.

John laughed. "I guess we don't, but don't get your hopes up with this house either, honey. Like you said, we aren't in a financial place to purchase. Things don't just magically work out."

He's wrong, Danyella thought. *Things do magically work out. Maya's taught me that life will provide what I desire. I just have to let it in.*

They wouldn't have gone to the house had John not wanted to get her out of her slump about the rental house. They wouldn't have spent so many glorious days waking up with such gratitude and joy for a new home if they hadn't felt the rental house was already theirs. Danyella thought that the universe had dangled a carrot in her face by thrilling her with something small only to give her something much better. She had felt the same way about her relationship with Maya; that pregnancy never brought her the type of relationship she had expected; instead, it brought her to the deepest relationship of her life. She didn't mind that John didn't understand the magic of the universe the way she did. As she held Ron's business card, she was positive her house was on its way.

CHAPTER 17

THE ART OF ALLOWING

"Wake up, meditate, and write as many positive-aspect lists as you can! Do it for thirty days and watch your life transform around you," Danyella had read in one of her favorite author's self-improvement books. "OK, sounds simple enough. I'm sure I can do it, right, Jonathan?" she playfully asked her son.

"Mama!" He ran to bask in her loving attention.

Meditating and focusing on writing such lists in the morning meant waking up before Jonathan did. The first few days, she was tempted to hit snooze when her phone alarm announced it was time to get out of bed, but then she remembered her author's advice: "If you set your alarm earlier to start this new morning ritual, your ego will tempt you to stay in bed. But if you value your happiness and health, your determination will override your ego. You're stronger than your ego and your snooze button!" She groaned and rolled out of bed without looking too long at Jonathan, which would have made her want to snuggle with him.

She put her hair in a bun and went to the living room. She sat on a pillow, crossed her legs, and put her thumbs and middle fingers together with her palms facing the sky. She wasn't sure what the finger placement meant; she just knew it was what people did when meditating.

The first few days of her new routine had been harder than she had expected. She initially was frustrated when she tried to quiet her mind. *Just shut up!* she told it one morning while trying to focus on nothing as the book had instructed. On the fifth day, she felt like she was wasting her precious morning hours on something that didn't seem to be working, but she wasn't the type to give up easily; she continued in determination with the routine.

The second week, she was still struggling to stop her thoughts. Meditation wasn't bringing any profound messages, and she wasn't feeling any out-of-body experiences that she had read about, but her life outside meditation started to change. She slowly started noticing a difference in the way she felt during the day, and soon enough, things started happening to her. It began with little things like finding front-row parking everywhere she went; it was as if someone was saving the best parking spots for her, but she didn't give this parking luck too much thought until bigger desires started raining in.

On a walk one sunny spring morning while she was pushing Jonathan in his too-tiny umbrella stroller, a new desire sparked in her mind. "Mommy wants a nice new jogging stroller that will fit you comfortably." Jonathan just smiled at his mom. "I guess if it's meant to be, the money will come."

Going about her day, she forgot about her request for the new stroller. It wasn't until the following week when she was flipping through a magazine that her eyes caught an ad for a jogging stroller and she started daydreaming about one imagining what it would feel like jogging behind it. She saw Jonathan taking a midmorning nap in it during their long morning jogs.

Someone honking outside interrupted her fantasies; Jonathan looked up at his mom for some assurance about the noise. "It's OK, honey! It's almost time for Daddy to come home. Maybe that's him." She looked through the living room window and saw Jacky unloading a practically new jogging stroller from the bed of her pickup. Danyella's energy jumped. She heard her niece and nephew bantering about who was going to ring the doorbell first as they raced up the stairs to her apartment. She turned to Jonathan, who was then standing next to the couch still trying to figure out what the noise meant. She swooped him up and plopped him on her hip. "Your cousins are here!"

Jonathan's eyes sparkled at the sight of Mackenzie and Isaac jumping up and down when his mother opened the door. "We have a present for you!" they chimed in unison. Jonathan gleefully wiggled at the excitement of his cousins. Danyella enjoyed the zest that her niece and nephew always brought; it was easy to get excited around them.

"We found you an amazing stroller!" Jacky shouted as Danyella and Jonathan made their way down the steps followed by Mackenzie and Isaac.

"It's beautiful! Just what I've been wanting! How did you know? Where'd you get it?"

"We found it on the side of the road with a free sign on it," Ben, Jacky's husband, said sounding astonished and a little annoyed at the same time.

Danyella looked at her sister to check if Ben was being serious. Jacky smiled as if she'd just won the lottery and said, "It's true! I could hardly believe it! We were driving through that neighborhood at the top of the hill with the big houses to drop Mackenzie's soccer buddy off after practice, an—"

Ben butted in. "And your sister almost gave me a heart attack when she saw the stroller and screamed at the top of her lungs!"

Jacky rolled her eyes and laughed.

"I would've screamed too! This looks practically brand new!" Danyella said while placing Jonathan in the seat and buckling the straps.

"You two are sisters all right!" Ben joked.

The women looked at one another and winked.

"Uncle John!" Mackenzie shouted. Everyone turned to see John walking toward them with his lunch pail in hand and wearing his work badge.

"What's all the excitement about?" he teased.

Danyella quickly walked behind the stroller and began to push Jonathan toward him. "Look, honey!"

"That's really nice! You were just saying you wanted one of those the other week, right?"

"Yes I was, and here it is! All I do is want something, have confidence that it's coming, and wait for the universe to hand it over." Danyella smiled.

"Really?" Isaac said, looking confused while remembering all the, *You have to work hard to get what you want* talks his parents had given him. Danyella look cautiously at Jacky as not to step on their parenting toes before answering his question honestly.

"Yes, I believe we can have anything we desire, but we have to believe that it's going to be ours. If you have even an ounce of disbelief, it might not come true."

Isaac looked at his aunt in wonderment and then at the stroller and Jonathan bobbing up and down. It was as if everyone saw Isaac's brain absorbing a new concept right before their eyes. "And that is how you made this stroller happen for free?" he asked.

Ben jumped in. "Aunt Danyella didn't make anything happen. It was just a coincidence that she wanted something that we found for free, Isaac."

Danyella just smiled sweetly at her niece and nephew knowing that some people weren't ready to believe in their own power, and she was OK with that. But she knew that her new beliefs were powerful, that she had created this stroller, and she didn't need anyone to confirm that.

That was only the beginning of her desires being fulfilled. The following week, John came home with an unexpected bonus in addition to his paycheck. "A little gratitude to show our employees how thankful we are for all their hard work," the president of John's company had said while handing out the bonus checks.

Danyella looked at the amount of the bonus; it was the exact amount she had written down on her desire list. "Wow! I'm good!" she whispered feeling more powerful than ever.

"What was that?" John asked.

143

Danyella nervously brushed her hair back; she nervously wondered how to respond, but without giving it too much thought, she blurted out, "I said, 'Wow! I'm good!' I meant at attracting this money."

John scrunched his face in confusion waiting for her to confess that she was just joking. "What do you mean?" he asked laughing.

"I've been focusing on the things I desire with positive expectations about them, and they just keep showing up like magic. The stroller and then this!" As soon as she told the truth, she wished she had fibbed.

John's expression was a mix of disbelief and humor. "You're so cute, honey! I think you're reading too much into things," he said condescendingly.

Danyella brushed that off and changed the subject to what they would do with their new money. Tapping into the joy of the desire that had just arrived was exciting; she forgot all about a new house.

Taking a vacation had been on her mind as long as she could remember, but she was surprised when John said, "Let's go to Hawaii for your birthday!" the next night.

"Really? You sure?" Danyella said, nervously thinking of the cost.

"This is the perfect time with your birthday coming up and the bonus," John said.

She couldn't argue with that; there couldn't be a more perfect time and circumstance. So they set the dates. When Danyella was online buying the tickets, she looked up in the sky, as if Maya was hovering above her, and winked. It was another thing she could scratch off her list of her desires. *Maya, with all these desires flowing in …* She paused; she wondered if she could finish her question without getting too emotional. … *does this mean you and Sofia will be arriving next?* She wanted an instant response. Her thoughts were quiet. A little too quiet. No response arrived, but she was in such a state of joy that she felt as if all her desires were already there, so she let her worries about Maya not coming to earth anytime soon float away. She remembered what Mrs. Mooney, her third-grade teacher, had repeatedly told her: "Everything in divine timing, my dear." Her favorite teacher's advice calmed her. *Everything in divine timing, girls.*

With so many new things going on, Danyella and John had been too busy to worry about getting into a house, so she was surprised when Ron called and in a cheerful voice said, "I have some great news! If you and John are still interested in the house on Twenty-Second, the owners just dropped the price."

Danyella's momentary excitement at the news was quickly overshadowed by what she had previously convinced herself of. "I'm not sure if we're prepared to buy it," she said sadly.

"I understand, but I've been in the real estate business long enough to have learned that the majority of people are far better off and more prepared than they realize to purchase a home. Something tells me this house is for you."

Danyella smiled at the divulging of Ron's intuition; he had her attention. Going with a gut feeling was something Danyella hadn't expect from Ron. That prompted her to lower her mental barriers and begin to take him seriously. "I guess there's no harm in finding out what it would take to buy it," she said nervously.

"Let me run some numbers and see if they fit your income and budget. If not, no harm done, right?" Ron asked enthusiastically.

"Yes, I guess I'd never looked at it that way." Danyella felt enlightened.

John had heard her side of the conversation and playfully asked, "So we're buying a house?"

"We could be," she replied finding herself more excited about the possibility than she had thought she would be. John's face showed his concern, which inspired hers. "There are a lot of things we'd need to get done. I think it might take a miracle!" Her worries circled back around. She felt the contrast between her two emotions. She much preferred being excited and hopeful about buying this home than feeling pessimistic and worried about it. She remembered her magic in finding things to feel good about and started a conversation with John that headed in that direction. "What was your favorite part of the house, honey?"

"*Hmmmm* ... There are so many good things ... but I'd have to say that the garage was my favorite. So spacious ... It would fit all my tools as well as the cars."

She felt John's excitement rising.

"What about you, honey?"

"My favorite part is the goldfish pond. It was so calming, peaceful, and unique. I'd never seen anything like it before."

"You're right about that. Can you imagine us living there? We could just step out our front door and fish for our meals!"

That caused Danyella to choke on her orange juice and then laugh. "Honey!"

"No, not those sweet little goldfish!" John's laugh prompted Jonathan to laugh too.

Danyella couldn't wait to share all her fun with Kiki; texting about all the magic was nowhere near as fun as talking about it in person. The two had agreed to meet weekly at a neighborhood park to get some exercise and catch up with one another.

Danyella's list of new things she had manifested was so long that she worried about forgetting to tell Kiki something important, so she wrote them all down while sitting with Jonathan, who was watching his afternoon sing-a-long show. She flipped to the first blank page of her notebook and wrote, "My Magic." She smiled as she wrote each item down, and she laughed when she swiftly got to the bottom of the page. "That was quick!" Danyella announced.

Jonathan looked at her and smiled as if to reflect her joy. When she was happy, he lit up like a light bulb. When she laughed, he did too regardless of his ability to understand what she was laughing about. She recognized this pattern as she felt a rush of happiness. Jonathan stood up and wrapped his hands around her neck and said, "Lub you, Momma." Danyella's smile widened. She set her journal and pen down to nuzzle him into her sweet embrace. *I'm the luckiest mom in the world! There's nothing better than this!*

She thought of Maya and Sofia, which seemed to beckon them. She felt their presence around her and Jonathan, and her heart felt complete; she felt that she was hugging all three. Time felt as if it had slowed down; she wanted to stay in this magnified feeling forever. Like a light bulb being switched on, Danyella felt a knowingness that space and time were just mirages and that being with or without someone was just a state of mind. She had read about soulmates being physically distant but emotionally together; she felt that neither space nor time could distance her from her children. Worlds, realms, and lifetimes of separation didn't affect the time they were now experiencing together; nothing seemed more real than this.

She returned to her notebook and went to the first page; she saw a list she had written down almost a year earlier. She looked at the date trying to spark a memory of writing it, but nothing surfaced. She didn't remember writing that list, but she clearly had. The page was titled in her handwriting My Top Ten Desires. It was a window into her past mindset. *What did I want then?*

For a moment, she thought her eyes were playing tricks on her. It was almost identical to the list she had just written. She flipped to her "My Magic" list. Her eyes hadn't deceived her ... The lists were almost exactly the same she realized as she flipped back and forth between the two lists. Her heart sang knowing that she had deliberately allowed some of her most exciting wishes into her present experience.

She stopped on the last three items on her list of desires, which weren't on her new list: "A house ... Maya ... Sofia." She took a deep breath. *The house might be on its way, girls!* She paused. *Does this mean you two might be next?* Danyella was overjoyed at the thought of her daughters joining her on earth.

Just then, she heard a frog croaking outside their apartment. *A frog? Here?* Jonathan began to jump up and down with glee. "What is it, baby boy?" she asked in her sweetest voice.

"Rib rib!" he shouted joyfully. Danyella tried to decode his baby language. "Rib rib!" He shouted again and burst into laughter, which made her laugh too.

"What does 'Rib rib' mean?" she asked in between laughs, but Jonathan just continued to hop up and down excitedly. She scanned his toys trying to see what he might be imitating, and she heard a lullaby playing on TV: "Ribbit ribbit goes the frog!"

"Rib rib!" he shouted even louder at the sight of the frog on TV.

"You're saying, 'Ribbit ribbit,' like the TV frog, honey!" she said with satisfaction at understanding what he was trying to say. The goose bumps she felt brought her back into focus. *Three frogs in a row. What are you trying to tell me, Maya?* Nothing floated into her mind. She had been communicating with Maya for so long that she knew Maya preferred to tell her some things directly, but other things, she encouraged Danyella to find. *Let's see what good old Google says.* Danyella's eyes widened as her internet search resulted in the words, "Prosperity, good luck, and fertility." *I am on a good-luck streak lately. Does this mean I will experience fertility soon, baby girl?*

Later that week, Danyella and John enthusiastically scurried to finish everything Ron had told them to do to see if they qualified to purchase the house. "At the very least we'll find out how far away we are from buying a house, right?" she asked him one evening. "Not that I'm the type who thinks of things at the very least, of course."

John laughed. "You got that right!"

"Things are going too darn well for us not to believe it's all coming together for a reason, like our buying-our-first-house kind of reason!"

"They are coming together pretty nicely and in a way we'd never expected."

John paused awkwardly, which prompted her to ask, "But ...?"

"I just don't want you to get your hopes up about this house, honey. I don't want you too excited because it's not a reality yet," he said as if giving her a lecture about being practical.

She remembered when she used to think about things that way too. "Don't count your chickens till they hatch!" her parents had told her when she was a child. It wasn't until she met Maya that she could even fathom enjoying something that hadn't manifested in her physical world yet, but Maya had changed all that by bringing to life a sort of excitement about things not yet created. She had shown Danyella that there was beauty in the journey to things and that sometimes, the journey was juicier than what she had wanted in the first place. She couldn't physically hold the keys to her new house, but she felt energy pulsing through all the events leading up to this house. She was enjoying the journey to her house, and she knew that was the important part. It didn't matter where they ended up as long as they were happy along the way. *How boring would it be to enjoy only the things we already have? Once they're here, they're old news, and then we want different things.* She had never felt more clear about the truth. She felt that Maya was patting her on the back for a thought well done.

"I understand your concern, honey," she told John. "But I promise it'll all work out as it's supposed to. If this house doesn't work out, there'll be another. I'm just excited about the process."

John's face turned from concern to relief; he gave her a hug and said, "OK, good!"

She felt his love for her even if it did show up in his reactions to his fearful thinking. She believed that there was no right or wrong way of looking at things. Instead, she had discovered that when her thoughts felt good, it was because she was looking at things in a better direction, and when she felt bad, it was because she was holding herself apart from the good that life had to offer. She also knew not to take advice from those who were offering it out of their fears.

She wanted John to believe all she had learned, but she knew that words didn't teach and that this good-feeling perspective was something only experience could provide. For Danyella, Maya had been that experience. Being able to reach for the best-feeling thought in any situation was a perspective Danyella was enjoying in almost everything she did. The more she focused on what felt good, the more good things she found to focus upon; they seemed to come one after another. She was finding it easier to look at what was going right. She knew that what was right in front of her was reality but that it wasn't necessarily what she needed to focus on to get where she wanted to be.

The next morning, she felt the dull pain of cramps. She pulled her knees to her chest and tried to rub the tiredness out of her eyes. *I guess it's about that time.* She grabbed her phone to check the date and smiled when she saw it was the twenty-second. "Hi, baby girl!" she said as if Maya were near. *This feels so familiar.* She opened her ovulation app, and her heart sang when she realized that her last three periods had arrived on the twenty-second. *That's why it feels so familiar! I got excited the last couple of months at the realization that my period had arrived on our day, baby girl!*

She felt a joy that didn't seem to be just hers. She knew that Maya and Sofia were as excited as she was. Nothing Danyella had experienced had been as fulfilling as her relationships with her children, even the ones her arms ached to hold.

Danyella's focus remained on the positive things in her life. The journey to her house was one of them. Every step Ron asked them to take in preparation seemed easy and effortless. Danyella felt sure of the direction they were going even if it was full of first times and unknowns. She felt Maya nudging her with confidence with each decision she made. The number twenty-two showed up on paperwork, totals, and brochures, which made her feel safe. She felt that she had a personal guide pointing her in the right direction with each step. That evening when her phone ring, something told her that the call was about the house.

"Hi, Danyella! It's Ron, with some great news!"

"Hi, Ron! Great! What's the good news?" she said loud enough to catch John's attention.

"You two have been preapproved for the purchase price, so I sent to the sellers the offer we previously wrote up. I received a quick response." He paused.

Danyella's eyes brightened while locked on John's. "Yes?"

"They accepted it! Congrats!"

"Seriously?" Danyella gasped. John walked closer wanting to hear more of the conversation.

"Yes, seriously! I'll send over some of the finalizing paperwork you need to sign, but it looks like if everything goes well, you could be in your new house by next month."

"Thank you so much, Ron!"

"You're welcome! My pleasure. You must have had a magic spell on this house or something. I've never seen a house deal work out quite the way this one has."

His words about magic echoed in her mind. It had felt like magic to her as well, except she knew that the world was filled with this sort of magic and that everyone had access to it at any time. If it could be found in the wretched pain of a mother who had lost a child, she was sure that this magic could be found anywhere for those who sought it.

The house closed quickly, and suddenly, Danyella and John were holding the keys to their first home. They were overjoyed as they packed up their apartment. Even when cleaning the apartment, they found themselves laughing and kissing. Danyella felt that someone had orchestrated the perfect plan to lead her to her happiness. It was better than she could have planned herself.

Looking around the kitchen in the apartment, she remembered all the joyful meals and the endless banana bread muffins she had baked with love and even her many battles with morning sickness. The living room still held the energy of their laughter and the excitement they felt each day when John arrived home from work. She smiled as she thought about bringing Jonathan home from the hospital. She thought about her painful loss when she was bleeding on the bathroom floor but then about Maya's joyful presence since then.

"You about ready?" John asked interrupting her stream of grateful thoughts. He stood in the hallway holding their final box of stuff.

"As ready as I'll ever be," Danyella said while looking at the empty walls.

"Meet me in the car after you lock up," John said knowing Danyella was always emotional with goodbyes and even goodbyes to places.

"Goodbye, old friend." Danyella said as she switched off the hall light and gazed at the empty living room one last time. Withdrawing the key from the lock, she felt a tingle on the back of her neck. She knew that Maya, Sofia, and her angels were applauding her on this last step toward the next chapter in her life.

The next morning, Danyella, John, and Jonathan woke up in their new home, which made them all feel brand new. The house echoed with emptiness as most of the furniture was still in the garage. The smell of fresh paint made the established house feel new. The excitement of decorating their new space urged Danyella to quickly eat breakfast and get to work. Jonathan enjoyed trailing in and out of the boxes as Danyella emptied each one. The house slowly began to come alive with their belongings. Danyella reveled in designing the look of the new space. She had a swiftness and flow about her that was there only when she was enjoying something.

After placing the last book on the bookshelf, she stepped back to admire her work. The large living room seemed complete. She was feeling the benefits of her creation. *We did good, huh, baby girl?* A buzzing noise on a living room window caught her attention. She turned and saw a bumblebee buzzing on the glass. *There you are, Maya!* she thought while smiling at the sight of her daughter's symbol. Her heart felt full.

CHAPTER 18

ALMOST THERE

All the excitement of getting settled in their new house made the weeks fly by. It was suddenly July. To celebrate Independence Day, the family of three went on vacation to Huntington Beach, California, the perfect setting for the holiday. The warm sun glistened on the skin of all the beachgoers while the waves sparkled as they crashed on the shore. Danyella took in the summer scene unfolding around her—the families setting up their beach chairs and barbecue grills. Danyella felt grateful, knowing her family was getting to spend the holiday in such a beautiful place. She scurried to unpack so she could take Jonathan down to the water. John began to set up their grill to prepare for lunch.

Safely in his mom's arms, Jonathan watched as the shore flipped and tossed water onto his mother's toes. He giggled each time it arrived at her feet. Danyella began to playfully run away from the water as it approached, while laughing and clenching Jonathan tightly when the water caught her feet anyway.

John smiled as he watched them from his beach chair under the umbrella. He remembered Danyella before Jonathan had arrived and his wish to fulfill her biggest desire ... the pain they had suffered when it wasn't filled time and time again ... her brokenhearted look every month her period came ... his desperate prayer to give her a child. The memories seemed so far away at that point, something from a distant world, and he was thankful. Watching his wife and son play on the beach sparked a deep appreciation for the abundant joy they felt. *Thank you!* he thought not sure whom he was thanking. *God?* He wasn't sure what he believed in, but he knew that in his own way, he had begged someone to give them a child, and that request had been granted. He was grateful.

Danyella and Jonathan came back to their fortress in the sand. The sun had turned their cheeks pink, and it wasn't even noon. John was micromanaging the grill; he loved barbecuing and enjoyed the look on Danyella's face when she tasted his perfected recipe.

Danyella lathered more sunscreen on herself and Jonathan and sat under their oversized umbrella to get some shade. Jonathan wiped his eyes and reached for Danyella's arms to cuddle. She smiled and complied with his request. "Let's take a rest, baby," she said as she leaned back onto the bundle of beach towels. Jonathan didn't protest; he nuzzled in her embrace and fell fast asleep. The sight of her baby peacefully resting filled her with satisfaction. Any time she thought about being his mother, she thought about Maya and Sofia too. She smiled and looked up, as if she might see them someplace in the sky. She saw a plane with a banner stringing behind it with an ad of some sort meant for the beachgoers. She squinted her eyes to read it: Bumblebee 9/22 Coming Soon! Believing she had read it incorrectly, she gently unloaded Jonathan from the crook of her arm and sat up to make sure she wasn't dreaming. Her eyes hadn't deceived her; she'd read it correctly. She felt an old, familiar spark of love that she often felt when she received signs from Maya, which always struck her with overwhelming worthiness and gratitude. *All this for me?* She quietly shed tears of love as she soaked up the beauty of the moment.

The rest of the day was spent enjoying John's amazing barbecued chicken wings, relaxing under the sun, and chasing Jonathan down the shore. That night, they and everyone else there enjoyed the colorful fireworks, but Danyella couldn't stop thinking of the banner. *Can this be really happening? Of course it is!* Her heart sang. She felt sure. She wanted to scream in joy, but she settled for a large smile and hugging Jonathan tightly instead. She kept the reason for her excitement to herself.

The vacation and holiday had renewed Danyella. Waking up early for meditation that Monday was easy. As soon as the light hit her eyes, she leaped out of bed to find what the day would bring. She tiptoed out of the bedroom, grabbed her crystals from the bowl on the windowsill, and snuggled down on a pillow on her living room floor facing the sunshine that was stretching across the floor. Even the silence seemed to bring up thoughts. One after another, she hushed them. Focusing on the in and out of her breath helped.

Before she knew it, the timer on her phone rang to remind her that even meditations have endings. She stretched her arms and smiled as she looked around her beautiful home. It still hadn't quite sunk in that she was sitting in the living room of one of her largest dreams.

She felt an urge to do something with her gratitude. *But what?* Normally when she was thankful for something, she would send a thank-you card to whomever had given it to her, and she wished she could thank someone for all the joy that came with her new home. *Why not write the universe a thank-you card?* she heard in her mind. *You're right, Maya!*

The moment her pen hit the card stock, it started dancing. "Thank you for my house. Perfectly placed in a friendly and safe neighborhood and close to many of our favorite places. Thank you for our neighbors. Thank you for all the welcoming waves we receive every day when we see them ..." The gratitude she felt was a lightning bolt running through her body. "Thank you for those who designed and built this house. Thank you for its gorgeous colors of emerald pine, taupe, and charcoal ..." She thought that she would have never combined those colors for this house, and she fantasized about what colors she would have painted the exterior of the house if she could have had a choice. *Maybe a blue-grey.*

But then she felt the familiar warmth of external chatter: *There is great purpose in the colors of your house.* She paused; she was still trying to get used to receiving direct guidance from beyond. No matter how many times she had communicated with Maya that way, she felt strange about receiving a direct response to her thoughts. *What do the colors represent?* she asked. *Healing,* she heard. She was overcome with emotion. Her eyes welled up, and her throat tightened. She felt more connected with life than she had ever before. She smiled at these beautiful messages, beautiful gifts that had started with Maya and that seemed to connect her to every part of her life. She knew it felt right, pure, and positive; she knew she wasn't just making it all up.

Her phone jolted her back to reality. *I almost forgot I was on earth!* It was a text from Kiki: "Something told me to send you this song. Not sure why. When you figure out what it means, let me know. XOXO Kiki." *Interesting,* Danyella thought. She pushed the play link and waited; she was soon listening to an unfamiliar song dazzle her ears. She smiled as she wondered why Kiki would have sent her such an unusual song. "We are almost there. How wonderful our love will be, for you and for me. Almost there, where we will share our dream come true. Love has waited such a long time, now we are only a kiss apart," she heard. Her hands began to tremble; she had an undeniable feeling that the song was from Maya. Her mind sifted through the lyrics. Maya was telling her that she was on her way. Danyella cried tears of pure joy that washed away years of being separated from Maya. She felt a wholeness that she hadn't felt since her miscarriage, like something coming full circle that had stretched on for longer than desired. *We're finally going to be together, baby girl! The greatest gift!*

How long ago was my last period? She grabbed her phone and searched for the calendar. Her eyes rapidly scanned the dates on the calendar counting the weeks back to her last period: *One ... two ... three ... four! This means I can take a test!*

She heard Jonathan waking up in the other room and found him sitting up in bed with a beaming smile and a head full of bed-head hair. "Did you sleep well, my love?" He reached out his arms for her. Holding her not-so-little baby anymore, she whispered, "Your sister's on her way! We'll surprise daddy!"

Danyella felt so confident about her communication with Maya that she didn't think she needed a pregnancy test to confirm it, but she knew that John would need some proof. So that afternoon she rummaged through the bathroom cabinets for the box of pregnancy tests. She grabbed one that reminded her of the times when the tests had given her a different feeling, usually fear. She smiled. Her new reality was far more enjoyable than the one she had allowed her past to be.

While following the routine of the test's steps, she started counting the endless ways she could tell John and her parents about the pregnancy. The idea of that Promoted to Big Brother T-shirt came to mind. Danyella put the pregnancy stick on the bathroom counter and ran off to locate the shirt in Jonathan's dresser. The ducky pajamas seemed to jump out at her as she flipped through the clothes and made her smile knowing that they had always been meant to be filled. *Now they'll be filled twice!* She found the Promoted to Big Brother shirt and held it up to gauge its size—*Perfect for Jonathan now! You sneaky universe!*

Right before she returned to the bathroom, Danyella felt fear creep in. *What if I misunderstood your signs, Maya? What if this is all too good to be true?* she asked herself. *Have faith in your inner guidance,* she felt Maya reply. Danyella took a deep breath as she remembered all that Maya had brought into her life. The understanding that life always turned out the way it was supposed to ... the understanding that the universe always had a plan better than any of hers ... knowing there was magic in everything if she was willing to find it. *You're right, baby girl. I just have to have faith.* She felt joy returning, and she picked up the pregnancy test. Danyella's face flushed at the sight of the word *Pregnant* on the test screen. She knew she had heard Maya correctly. She was holding the proof.

Danyella had dreamed of Maya joining her on earth so many times, and it finally was becoming reality. She looked at her reflection in the mirror and saw versions of her past self along with her now joyous self merging together. She could feel the memories of standing in front of the mirror with a pregnancy test in hand, sorrow in her mind, tears in her eyes, and faith in her heart that someday she would be experiencing this very moment. She put her hands on her belly and said a little prayer: *Thank you, Love, for this great blessing! Please guide me through this pregnancy, and keep my child safe.*

That afternoon, Danyella couldn't wait for John to arrive home from work. She dressed Jonathan in the big brother T-shirt and wondered how long it would take John to notice. "You look handsome, big brother!" Danyella said while putting the shirt on her toddler. Jonathan looked down at the shirt, patted his chest in excitement, and turned around to see the baby in the mirror wearing the same thing. "Cheese!" he said as if he were getting his picture taken. Danyella giggled. "You're right, baby boy! This moment needs a picture. I want to remember this for the rest of my life." Danyella grabbed her phone and quickly snapped a photo.

She heard the swoosh of the front door opening and the thud of it closing. "He's home!" she whispered to Jonathan, who looked at her and relaxed at the sight of her cheerful body language. He ran out of the bedroom and into the living room with Danyella following not wanting to miss her husband's first glimpse.

"Hi, my beautiful family!" John said as if seeing them energized him.

"Daddy!" Jonathan said while holding his arms up toward him. Watching their daily reunion always made her smile and struck a warm chord of love in her heart.

"Something smells good! What's for dinner?" John asked as he leaned in for a kiss while holding happy Jonathan.

"Your favorite!"

"Steak?"

Danyella smiled in agreement.

"How did I get so lucky?"

Danyella smiled and awkwardly stared at wherever John's eyes went. John wondered why her gaze was constantly shifting. "Do you have a new shirt, buddy?" he asked. At the mention of his name and his shirt, Jonathan looked down at it drawing John's eyes to the words on it. "No way!" When Danyella nodded happily, he asked, "Are you really pregnant, honey?"

"Yes!"

"You are indeed promoted, Jonathan!"

The reveal was perfect, just how Danyella had imagined it.

Danyella loved the feeling of a new life bubbling in her. As her belly grew larger, so did the simpler perks of pregnancy including the kind gestures of strangers letting her cut in the grocery store lines, everyone always wanting to spoil her with food, and simply being able to relax after dinner with her tummy hanging out. Danyella also noticed that eating seemed to be a unique experience when she was pregnant; everything seemed to taste like the best food she had ever tasted.

Since John and Danyella had agreed on having only two children, she savored what seemed to be her last pregnancy and promised herself that she would enjoy it to the fullest. *A boy and a girl. Two is good enough for me,* she happily thought as she rubbed her expanding belly. She remembered Aunt Samantha saying that Maya and Sofia were planning to arrive. The thought of twins made her smile and encouraged daydreams of two of everything in pink. She could barely wait for her ultrasound, which would reveal just how many babies she was carrying.

CHAPTER 19

GIRL OR BOY?

Danyella felt like a kid waiting for Christmas to arrive the week before her gender-reveal party. Her mom had done a great job of keeping all the party details a secret, so Danyella could only imagine what the party would be like. She grinned as she thought about the shock most everyone would have when they realized she had been right about the baby being a female all along.

At night, Danyella would dream about the party, and in her dreams, it was not a pleasant affair. Things forgotten … the reveal gone wrong … In one dream, her mother didn't complete the reveal and just began to tell people that the baby was a boy. Danyella woke up confused by that one. *It must be my nerves getting the best of me.* She tried to push the dream far away from her thoughts, but in the next night's dream, she was anxious when she got to the gender-reveal party. She had no awareness that she was dreaming, but she felt the repetition of this unwanted place. She found herself standing in her mother's living room. Grey, lifeless decorations drooped from the ceiling. Her friends and family looked dull and uninterested in the gathering. They all stood in pairs and deep in conversations, hardly noticing Danyella.

She scanned their faces waiting for someone to make eye contact with her, but no one did. Finally, she saw Jacky beaming from across the room. Jacky approached Danyella with a small box in her hands. Danyella started to complain about the despair of the party. "Where's Mom? Why hasn't she told us what the sex of the baby is yet?" Danyella whined.

"I have someone I want you to meet!" Jacky said as she gave the box to Danyella, who didn't question the oddity of Jacky's words and her mismatched actions; instead, she opened the box and suddenly found herself inside the box, which was now the size of a large empty room. She stood all alone. She felt calmness radiate through her body; she stayed with the feeling for several moments before the movement of cotton on her arm made her look down and see a baby wrapped in a white cotton blanket in her arms. She stared into the baby's eyes searching for familiarity; this visitor felt new and strange. The baby was oddly quiet and bashful and seemed to be trying to figure out who she was.

When she asked, "Who are you?'" the baby's eyes twinkled. "What's your name?" When the baby opened his mouth to answer, a loud, annoying alarm screeched. Jolting awake, she realized that her alarm had gone off right at the most important part of her dream. She rubbed her eyes and pushed back her hair. She tried to recall each detail of the dream so she wouldn't forget any. She wished she could go back to her dream. She liked the warmth and comfort she felt when holding the baby. But it didn't feel like Maya or Sofia. *Who was this dream visitor? And what does this dream mean?*

The day of the party, Danyella was thankful to wake up from no dreams at all. She had pushed the previous dreams out of her mind so she could focus on her thrill at the unveiling of Maya joining her on earth, something she felt she had waited her whole life for. She danced as she got herself and Jonathan ready. Danyella had bought a maternity shirt that read, Pink or Blue, No Matter Which, We Love You! the week before and wore it that day to not be overzealous with her unshakable knowledge she was carrying her daughter.

At her mother's house, she was greeted with pink and blue streamers lining the walls and the sweet smells of popcorn and cake tickling her nose. She smiled at how much thought her mom had put into throwing this beautiful party.

"Hi, Danyella!" her cousin Christy squealed as she walked into the room.

"Hi, Christy!" Danyella said as she embraced her cousin.

"So what's your guess?" Christy asked.

"I already know it's a girl," Danyella said confidently.

"That's why I'm wearing pink too! I had a strong feeling with mine too. A mother's intuition is stronger than anyone else's guess."

The house quickly filled with guests. Once everyone had settled in, Danyella's mom announced, "Thank you everyone for coming to the big reveal of Danyella's and John's second baby! I know everyone can't wait to find out if it's a boy or girl, but I'll enjoy being the only one who knows that for a few more minutes." Danyella's mom giggled and winked at her daughter. "I have two dolls behind Danyella and John. One doll is dressed as a girl, and the other's dressed as a boy. While John and Danyella face you, I'll pick up the doll that is the gender of their baby and bring it to them. When I do, make all the happy or disappointed noises you want, OK?"

The excited crowd cheered, and Danyella thought, *This is fun!*

Danyella and John enjoyed watching the crowd go wild with excitement at whatever her mother was doing behind them. *They're getting awfully excited! It must be because it's a girl.* Danyella thought. Her mom walked in front of them with both dolls, and Danyella's heart skipped a beat and her hands began to tremble as she realized that all the years of twin signs were possibly pointing to this moment. Time slowed way down. Her mom handed the girl doll to Christy and the boy doll to Danyella and John. Danyella sat motionless with the boy doll in her hands.

"It's a boy!" the crowd screamed. Danyella's face turned pale almost as if she had seen a ghost. All she could do to not burst out in tears was to laugh. It was as if she were having two experiences at the same time—an outer experience of smiles and laughter and an inner experience of shock and disbelief. Danyella had never experienced such an emotional tug-of-war between how she felt and how she knew she needed to present herself.

She turned to John, who seemed to be filled with joy, which encouraged Danyella to hide her true feelings even more. The room felt small and suffocating. She wished she could be anywhere but there. She wanted to run away and hide her face and her true feelings from everyone. *What? How can this be? How could I have not seen this coming? Why do I feel such great disappointment? I'm an awful mother! I thought my baby girl was here to join me on earth? What's happening?*

Although Danyella was smiling, her body language was more transparent than she realized. John whispered, "You all right?"

It took everything she had not to burst into tears as she responded, "Yeah, I'm fine. We have another baby boy," she whispered and smiled. She was lying, but speaking positive words seemed to curb her urge to crumble.

Family members and friends whirled around the couple giving hugs and congratulations. Danyella put herself on autopilot and responded in a cheery tone, but when the last guest left, she looked at her mom and burst into tears.

"What's wrong, honey?" her mom asked as she gave her the type of hug only her mother could give.

"I really thought he was a girl!" Danyella sobbed.

"Oh sweetie! I thought for sure you were a boy, and you turned out to be just the perfect girl for me. Things always work out for the best."

Danyella had been living the best relationship of her life in secret; she had no way to explain her huge disappointment. She let her mom wipe her tears and her husband give her a pep talk about how this was the perfect outcome; she kept her pain deep inside.

The next morning, Danyella was more grateful than ever for being a stay-at-home mom. No job meant no people to lie to, no one to hide her feelings from. She didn't mind breaking down in front of Jonathan; his sweet face was more than accepting of everything that Danyella offered him. He was the perfect set of ears she needed when she felt she would burst if she didn't tell someone about the magic she was experiencing. But that day, it was as if someone had squeezed the magic right out of her.

She felt like she was mourning a death all over again, but she felt strange to be mourning someone who had never been born. She felt as if she had lost her closest friend … someone she talked with every day … someone who was with her no matter what. But she couldn't feel her daughter anymore. In fact, Danyella didn't feel like talking to Maya just then. The confusion this unplanned twist had caused left her feeling estranged from Maya and questioning her spiritual beliefs.

If I got my daughter's signs about coming wrong, what else did I misunderstand? And the twin signs. I must have made those up too. Maybe this whole time, I was just talking to myself and making up that someone was responding in my mind! At the thought of it all being a lie, Danyella felt a sharp pain of discord in her heart. *Maybe I'm crazy! Maybe that's why I didn't tell hardly anyone about this relationship because deep down, I knew it was all fake. A lie I made up to feel better about losing my baby. I am so dumb!*

Jonathan turned from his toys on the living room floor and looked up at his broken mother. Even to a toddler, she didn't seem like herself. Her eyes were puffy, and her hair was a tangled mess. She looked grey and lifeless to him. He was too little to understand the sadness he saw in his mother, but just like anyone else, babies can feel when of something is wrong.

He walked to his weeping mother and put his hands on her knees, which interrupted her mental chatter and pulled her back to the present. She looked at Jonathan's loving face and saw his longing for her health and happiness in his eyes. She smiled and wrapped him up in her arms.

It was almost as if Jonathan were saying, *It's gonna be OK, Momma. I'm proof that everything works out for the best.* Danyella enveloped her mind and heart in that thought, which felt miles apart from the painful thoughts she had been drowning in moments ago. The better feeling was a sign to Danyella that she was starting to think of things in the right direction. "Thank you for the reminder, baby!" she whispered as she hugged her sweet boy.

That evening when John got home, Danyella's eyes were swollen red from her day of tears. "Honey!" he said sympathetically as he pulled her in close for a hug. "It's just a boy, not an alien," John said trying to sound comical.

She buried her face in his chest and tried to gain the courage to tell him the truth about Maya. After a long, comforting hug, Danyella pulled away and bit her lip. "Honey, I have to tell you something."

"Is everything all right?" John asked sounding worried.

"There's a lot I haven't told you about this baby. I don't even know where to start." John's confused look got Danyella to hurry to the point. "So this is gonna sound weird, but I've been talking to our baby's soul since we lost her three years ago." Danyella paused.

John wasn't sure how to respond to that. "Like on a Ouija board?"

She started nervously picking up Jonathan's toys to avert her gaze as she continued to explain. "No. I can hear the baby in my mind." It sounded as strange as it felt to say it out loud. John sat and waited for her to continue. She took a deep breath. It was harder to explain to him than she had expected. "Ever since I got pregnant the first time, the baby has been finding ways to communicate with me. It started with the due date showing up everywhere. Then it just evolved into symbols I'd see. Now, I can hear her and she can hear me." Danyella started to weep. "She's been telling me that she was coming. I was thrilled when I found out I was pregnant, and then when I found out that this baby is a boy ..."

She couldn't finish the sentence, but she didn't have to. John could fill in the rest. He didn't see the world the way she did. He was scared to ask any more questions. He was nervous about her telling him more that he didn't understand. So instead of trying to relate to or comfort his wife, he asked, "Are you sure it's not just your way of coping with the loss? I know it was very hard on you."

It took everything Danyella had not to break down and run to the other room, but after his response, she knew better than to say any more. She believed that there were two kinds of people—those who believed in the before and after lives and those who didn't, and now she knew which type her husband was. She felt guarded toward him in a way she never had; she tried to conceal the pain of not just one loss but also now a second but more subtle loss of the connection and solace she used to find in their marriage. She stared at her husband and said, "Yeah, maybe," which sounded as phony as it felt.

After putting Jonathan to sleep that night, she didn't snuggle up on the couch next to John as usual; she quickly got ready for bed. She felt emotionally and physically exhausted. She even slipped into bed without saying goodnight to John. She didn't want to think of herself as mad at him because he hadn't done anything that she hadn't been half-expecting, but she did feel the discord of betrayal; she felt something was dividing them. Normally, she didn't care what he believed, but it felt as if his not believing in her connection with their baby meant he also didn't believe she was telling the truth. To Danyella, that felt like he didn't believe in her. That thought weighed heavily on her heart. She wanted to cry, but the day of tears had exhausted her. She was tired of thinking about it, and she knew the quickest way to relieve her feelings of separation was to fall asleep. So she did.

John, being stressed out himself, stayed up late watching TV in the living room. Eventually, he noticed that his wife hadn't joined him on the couch or said good night. No light was shining from under their bedroom door, so he tiptoed in and saw her asleep.

Returning to the couch, he thought about how puffy her eyes had been when he had gotten home that day. He sighed thinking about their conversation and her expression when he told her she might have been making it all up. *Talking to our baby? That doesn't sound real.* He felt the tug-of-war between their opposing beliefs. He wished he could believe her, but his need for facts outweighed any desire to believe in the unseen. His frustration was more than he felt he could handle on his own, so he grabbed his phone and dialed his most trusted advisor, his dad. *He'll know what to say.*

"Hi, Pops ..." John said in a weary tone that his dad instantly picked up on.

"What's the matter, son?"

"Do you have a second? I need some advice."

"Sure thing. What are dads for?"

"It's Danyella. I'm not sure how to even talk about this. Uh, well, she told me tonight that she's ... that she thinks she can talk to our baby." He could instantly tell that his words didn't make sense to his dad.

"Talk to your baby? As in the unborn baby?"

"I know, I know. It sounds crazy. It *is* crazy. I feel that losing the first baby might have been too emotionally hard for her. And now, she's talking about communicating with the baby in her belly. I don't know, Dad. Do you think she's crazy?"

"That's a tough one, son. I've heard of people believing in all that spiritual connection stuff, but I'm not one of them. If you can't show it to me on paper, you might as well be making it all up. Maybe you should have her see a counselor or psychologist."

John felt fear creeping in due to his having shared Danyella's secret. His worry about what others might think had reemerged. He wasn't willing to admit it out loud, but he felt a truth in what

Danyella had told him even if he couldn't believe it all the way. He knew she wasn't crazy, but he couldn't disagree with his father thinking so either. He forced out the response he knew his dad would want to hear: "I agree she probably needs to get some professional help. She is going crazy. She seems to be losing her mind."

John ended the conversation nervously and turned off his phone. He turned around and saw a teary-eyed Danyella standing behind him in shock at the conversation she had overheard. Her face quickly changed from sadness to anger. "How could you share that information? Oh! So I'm crazy now? Is that what you think?"

John felt trapped. Without knowing what she had heard or what to say, he blurted out, "I'm worried about you, honey!"

Danyella rolled her eyes. "Worried, John? Really? Sounds to me that you're more worried about how to keep me *normal* in everyone else's eyes than how to understand me through your own!"

The silence spoke loudly. She wanted to run away, to be anywhere else than with this traitor. "Maybe you should go sleep at your parents'!"

John dropped his head, grabbed his coat and keys, and left their house. As soon as the door slammed behind him, Danyella dropped to her knees, grabbed her belly, and began sobbing violently.

CHAPTER 20

THE NAME

The next morning, Danyella woke up to the touch of Jonathan's hands on her cheeks. "Momma!" he said with glee as she slowly opened her tired eyes.

She had not slept much that night. Her pillow was still damp from a night of tears. "Hi, baby," she said while forcing a smile.

"Lub you, Momma!" Jonathan said while hugging her. If anyone could bring her out of her double heartache, it was her sweet boy. She kissed his head. For him and only him, she got out of bed. The sight of the sun sparkling felt to her like the universe trying to coax her out of her stubborn pain, but instead, she held onto it tightly. Normally, she would lift her spirits by confiding in Maya, but that morning, she was confused and felt estranged. She felt tricked. *What was all that "We'll be together soon" talk?* She busied herself with preparing breakfast for Jonathan, and when she couldn't stand her negative thoughts any longer, she decided to call her aunt.

"Aunt Samantha."

"My sweet Danyella! How are you, sweetheart?"

Danyella couldn't conjure up even one sentence that summed up how she was doing. She simply sobbed and hoped that her aunt would somehow rescue her from all her pain.

"Oh my sweet girl, all is well. Take a deep breath, take a seat, and tell me what's going on."

Danyella caught her breath. "So much has gone wrong! I don't know where to even start."

"Start with your heart, my love."

Danyella nodded as if her aunt could see her. "It's Maya. She told me she was coming. When I found out I was pregnant, I could feel her with me. Then I found out my baby is a boy! I'm so confused. Why would she tell me she was coming if she wasn't? And then I opened up to John about Maya, and he acted like I was crazy. I heard him talking to his dad last night saying I was crazy, so I told him to leave." Just talking about it lifted some of the weight she felt on her shoulders; she felt less alone.

"You need to speak to Maya, darling."

Danyella felt like a stubborn child not wanting to speak to a friend who had hurt her, but she knew her aunt was right. "I haven't spoken to Maya since I found out about the baby being a boy."

"I know, my dear. I can tell. Maya will tell you why. But instead of just talking through your thoughts as you normally do, write down your questions and allow her answers to flow through you in written form. I think this is important right now."

Danyella nodded again.

"And as for your husband, he's not like you, my dear. He's not as brave as you are when it comes to accepting things not seen, and he cares very much about what others think of you and him. Give him some space and time. If he was meant to join you on this journey, he will. But that's not up to you. It's up to him."

Her aunt's words made Danyella feel hopeful. "Thank you, Aunt Samantha," she said sniffling back her tears as she hung up.

What will I even say to Maya? It felt strange not to be talking to someone whom she had spoken to anytime she had wanted. Even relationships beyond the physical world seemed to have their ups and downs. And so just as with earthly relationships, she valued her relationship with her daughter and began to think of what to say and ask so they could heal this strain.

That afternoon when Jonathan was napping, she sat at her desk and said a little prayer: "Please bless my communication with Maya so I can rest my heart and mind. Give me the strength to ask the questions and listen to the answers my heart yearns for. Please help me do this with love, not resentment. Thank you. Amen."

She nervously gripped her pencil waiting for some profound way to start things off. Just the simple thought of what to say to Maya seemed to set off a sort of emotional beacon. She felt warm, loving energy all around her, and she heard, *Go ahead, Momma.* She exhaled and smiled at her daughter coaxing her to their reconciliation. Danyella started to write.

"Dear Maya, Mommy is confused by all of our previous communication. Please help me understand. Did I misunderstand your signs?"

175

"No" floated to her mind, and Danyella wrote it down as instructed by her aunt.

"So then you plan on joining me on earth?"

"Yes."

"Are you on your way right now?"

"I've always been on my way."

Danyella laughed thinking that Maya was enjoying not giving her a definite answer. She thought about how she could reword her question, but before she could, Maya interrupted her thoughts.

"All your desires have been granted and are on their way. Enjoy the journey. It's the journey that's delicious, not the result."

"But you still didn't answer my question, little girl!" Danyella said playfully while wagging her finger in the air. "Are you the baby in my belly?"

"You'll know I'm here when you hold me."

"But how will I know for sure?"

"You'll feel sureness. And if you doubt yourself, look for joy, who will be with you when I arrive."

Feeling the conversation had come to an end, Danyella eased back into her chair and let her hands drape like noodles towards the ground. She felt humbled. She knew Maya was right. She needed to enjoy her journey regardless of whether Maya would join her in this life. A new life was beginning, and it was a prize despite the details. *Just when I think I have life all planned out, I receive a curve ball, huh, little girl?* Danyella chuckled. Their conversation had lifted her spirits, just as she had hoped.

Danyella knew that John couldn't stay away forever and that her anger and dissatisfaction with him wouldn't last. But the angry part of her wanted to hold onto the betrayal she felt. Every night while she held their son and felt their unborn child stirring inside her, she ached for all she loved about John. She had never before experienced such a disconnection with him. The pain it caused was tearing her heart apart. More important, she worried about how this emotional strain might be affecting the baby in her belly. With all these thoughts stirring in her mind, she let her anguish silently flow out in her tears as she prayed to fall asleep.

After two days, John returned. They looked silently at one another as he entered the front door. Jonathan's excitement at seeing his daddy broke the awkward silence. Seeing Danyella's glowing face even if she was scowling at him made John's face soften. And hugging Jonathan seemed to make him want to forget all that had happened.

By nightfall, Danyella was willing to talk. With Jonathan fast asleep, they sat at the kitchen table and tried to find common ground. They swirled around their pain and confusion in conversation while John apologized profusely. They went to bed that night together, but as Danyella closed her eyes, she felt a separation in her emotions that she believed only time could mend.

The next day, Danyella felt a burning determination to heal. She wasn't sure how to do that, but she knew that Maya, her angels, and the universe would show her the way. And she was right. That afternoon, she was guided by an intense urge to meditate while Jonathan napped. She sat cross-legged with her hands on her swollen belly and relaxed into the rhythm of her breath. It wasn't long before she received the guidance she was expecting: *Make your heart so strong that you can lead rather than react to others around you. Become unshakeable.*

But where do I start?

Find and focus on that which feels good.

Danyella took the advice and began doing what came naturally to her; she made lists of things that felt good to think about. She cooked a wonderful dinner. Her new goal was to focus on feeling good, and that came easier than she had expected. She even stumbled upon books that outlined steps she could take to center her focus on joy. She felt like a college student immersing herself in a new theory about how to live. "Wake up in the morning and bask in gratitude for all that is around you and watch your days change …" she read. Such good advice resonated in her heart, and she felt that all her cells in her body were screaming "*Yes!*"

The next day on her weekly trip to the library with Jonathan, she felt Maya's guidance. Normally, Danyella would head to the third floor to hunt for children's books to read to Jonathan. But in the elevator, her eyes shifted to the fifth-floor button, which seemed to be urging Danyella to push it. She had gotten used to following such subtle signs pointing her in the right direction, so she pushed that button.

Exiting the elevator, she felt a sting of embarrassment as she pushed Jonathan's stroller into less-familiar territory that was thick with serious silence. Everyone there seemed very studious—men and women with their noses in books. *No babies*, Danyella thought. But no one seemed to notice Danyella, the stroller, or wide-eyed Jonathan. She nervously walked down an aisle as if she knew what she was looking for. She waited for something to jump out at her. *Heal* … The word flashed in her mind. She remembered the advice from her meditation about healing her heart. She quickly walked over to the self-help section and began to browse. She squealed with glee as several books seemed to find her, one right after another. Feeling satisfied with her loot, she joyfully walked back to the elevators and went down to the third floor. Jonathan's eyes lit up at the sight of the colorful building blocks and other children, and her eyes lit up at the sight of an opportunity to read while Jonathan played.

She flipped through one book letting her eyes land on whatever her angels knew she needed to read first. She liked the thought of coming across a page containing what her heart was searching for naturally. She stopped at a page that had a section on relationships. She rolled her eyes; she knew what Maya was getting at. Stubbornly not wanting to admit the truth, she knew that Maya was right. This pain with John didn't feel good, and so she knew she needed to focus on things about him that did feel good.

The book described an ancient belief about how people's perceptions controlled their outcomes. Danyella felt Maya staring over her shoulder. The pages talked about the immense control people had over their perceptions. "You have the choice to look at life and view it as a heaven or a hell," she read as her entire body felt the sting of truth. She thought about how recently she had been looking at John in a negative direction and how separate from him it made her feel. "The remedy is to find the positive in everyone and every situation. Find the positive and you will find the truth." The words *The remedy* stunned her. The advice seemed so simple yet so profound. *I'll do my best, Maya!*

Danyella practiced waking up in a state of gratitude just as she had read about the week before. The thought had intrigued her so much that she had put this newfound idea into practice. She found that she enjoyed starting her day by reveling in the goodness all around her. She began by opening her eyes and finding gratitude about the first thing she saw in the morning. Most mornings, the first lovely thing she saw was little Jonathan lying so sweetly on the other side of her bed, and her heart always flooded with joy at that sight.

Her next enjoyable thought she usually chose was her dogs snuggled at her feet. Third, she usually focused on how good it felt to lie in her warm bed.

One morning, she woke up in a different way. As she swept her hair from her eyes, something told her to keep her eyes closed. It was almost as if she weren't fully awake and her mind was far away from her body. Everything felt dark. The silhouette of a little boy began to appear. He was bashfully looking down. He was one of the most beautiful little boys she had ever seen. His black hair and light skin became prominent. He seemed to be two or three. Her mind's eye focused on the beauty of his perfectly pointed nose. That detail sparked a sudden connection; his nose was similar to hers. She soaked in the calm, loving, and perfect energy that felt so present.

She was pulled back to reality, and the image of the beautiful boy faded. She opened her eyes. Her mind ran circles around what had just happened. *That was my boy!*

She felt honored for having been given the chance to see his face; he was more breathtaking than she had imagined. He did look like her. Jacky's suspicions had been right. He also resembled little Jonathan. *Name him after you,* she heard.

Name him after me?

Name him Daniel.

Daniel ... She felt the importance of that name in her bones. She didn't know why or how, but she knew this new desire for his name had a great purpose.

CHAPTER 21

WHERE FOCUS GOES, ENERGY FLOWS

It had been three weeks since Danyella had overheard John talking with his father about her, but things weren't back to normal, at least not yet. They mimicked their old habits in many ways. Kissing hello and goodbye as they came and went … sitting down to dinner each night with Jonathan … making small talk about their days … but Danyella felt an uneasy sort of guardedness toward him. It was clear that she needed more than time to heal. She had put the advice of finding the positives in every situation into action except the one that pained her the most.

Alone in her bubble bath that evening, she thought about the lack of justice she felt regarding the situation with John.

Does that feel good to think about? Maya asked.

Danyella sighed. *No.* She thought about what she needed to do. *List things that feel good about John. Hmmm,* she thought while pressing her toe into the opening of the faucet. At first, her dissatisfaction for him fogged her mind about his positives. She had spent so much time looking at where he had gone wrong that she was out of practice looking at where he had gone right.

One, he's a good father. She waited a bit to see if Maya would help her with the list. *Two, I love how he makes special time just for Jonathan.* She smiled as she remembered the countless times her husband and son laughed uncontrollably while playing tag. *Three, I love how I can feel his love for me.* Her heart began to soften. *Four, I love how he worked so hard with me to create our beautiful boys.* Her list became easier. *Five, I love how he spoils me on my birthdays.* She looked at the watch on the counter; he had given it to her on her last birthday. *Six, I love how handsome he is no matter how mad I am at him.* She giggled. *Seven, I love how he adores me ... most of the time.* She tried to remember the last time he had shown his adoration for her, but that introduced more fog, and she was determined to stay positive. *Eight, I love how over the past thirteen years we've had an abundance of fun and loving and joyous memories.* The memory of a camping trip several years earlier that had gone terribly wrong but had brought them so much closer flashed in her mind. She smiled. *Nine, I love him more than I ever knew I could love a partner.* Her eyes filled with tears. *Ten, I can't wait to see him fall in love with you, Maya.* She began to feel centered again. She felt her love and faith in John regardless of how he was choosing to be. She knew with all her heart and mind that this was exactly the feeling she was meant to feel. It felt like clarity. It felt like ease. It felt like love.

Danyella watched those ten beautiful things multiply in her mind like wildflowers. It was surprisingly simple how everything had unfolded once she focused on the positives. She knew that he might do something she didn't desire some time or another, but that didn't matter. She had found her power in strengthening her positive thoughts and positive expectations of him, and that was all she had control over. With a heart so full, she felt satisfied. The ease Danyella found in shifting her beliefs about John felt great, and with her new beliefs came new actions. She felt a sort of lightness about things that she normally tried to control.

Though John usually kept things to himself, he also felt a shift in Danyella. He felt ready to do things he had wanted to do for weeks and thought she would finally receive them well. For a week straight, he came home from work with a bouquet of flowers for her. Each evening, Danyella got giddy when he came in with that day's flowers. She marveled at his thoughtful gesture and would playfully joke about her running out of places to put them.

One positive action led to another. He started leaving love notes for her to find that expressed his gratitude for her being a doting wife and loving mother. Love and gratitude overpowered any disappointments the past had written for them. Danyella felt her heart healing and knew that once again, Maya had helped her find her way.

As she blissfully meditated one Friday morning, she heard, *Believe in your ability to see the best in every situation.* Trying to keep the thought present, she recited it: *Believe in my ability to see the best in every situation.* She thought about that horrible week that had pushed her and John apart that was followed by Maya's instruction to focus on her good feelings and thoughts. She felt appreciation for all that followed between the two of them the previous week. She felt grateful. She felt healed. She felt complete.

With only six weeks left till her due date, Danyella's desire to hold her baby boy in her arms began to get the best of her. Every morning, she felt a burning desire for her pregnancy to end. It made her feel antsy, and her thoughts seemed to follow down the same path.

She dreamed about life with baby Daniel—baby naps, precious baby cuddles, and life slowing way down to welcome the new member of their family. She began to worry about how Jonathan might react to a baby intruding on his space and time. Her worry turned into fearful thoughts, and she started stressing over the inevitable changes her firstborn would shortly experience. *What if he feels ignored? What if he doesn't want to share me with the baby? What if he doesn't like the baby?* Her thoughts spiraled. But as usual, she heard Maya: *This new life arriving is a cocreation that includes Jonathan's desires too. Jonathan is a creator of his own life just as you are of yours. He requested Daniel along with you and John. Remember, we are all creators, no exceptions.*

Danyella was taken aback by Maya's wisdom. It was easy to forget that helpless babies were powerful creators too. This new awareness made her think of all the times she had tried to control circumstances for Jonathan not realizing that they were cocreating his life together. During all those moments of struggle for control, she had felt she was going about things in the wrong direction. This new belief felt good; it freed her from the burden of being solely responsible for how things turned out for her children. *Thank you, Maya!* Right then, baby Daniel kicked.

The understanding that Jonathan was his own creator inspired Danyella to enjoy the present. She thought about how these last few weeks would be the end of a special chapter in their lives; she would be the mother of two sons rather than one. Her focus changed from predicting when baby Daniel would arrive to enjoying every day with Jonathan. She wanted to soak in this soon-to-be forgotten way of life.

"What do you want to do with Mommy today?" she asked Jonathan at breakfast one morning.

"Run, Mommy!"

She smiled at his simple answer. "OK then. After breakfast, let's run!"

And they ran. They ran all around their house laughing and giggling.

"Chase me, Momma!"

She held one hand under her protruding belly and one hand out toward Jonathan as she ran laps around their happy home, giggling with her son. Jonathan had way more energy than his pregnant mom did. As she sat to rest, she continued to cheer her little runner on as his little feet stomped on the wood floor each time he passed her on the couch. She had forgotten all about the future and was enjoying the present just as she had intended.

Living in the present seemed to make time speed up for her. Days and nights became a continuum of happy moments strung together. She had almost forgotten her burning desire to know if Maya was planning on joining her on earth someday.

That night as she lay restless in bed next to John and Jonathan, she thought about her desires and wondered if Maya and Sofia were ever destined to join her in the physical world. She felt defeated with the thought of three pregnancies not yielding the results of her long-awaited Maya. *Maybe you're just meant to stay my guardian angel, huh, baby girl?* Her eyes welled up with tears for what she felt was a lost desire. Maya was silent.

A sharp pain rippled through her abdomen, tightening her nerves and alerting every cell in her body. She sat up and began to breathe heavily. *Here we go, baby Daniel!* She got up to prepare for the next contraction. She tiptoed to the bathroom not wanting to disturb her sleeping family. Memories of Jonathan's long labor inspired the thought, *Let them sleep. This might take a while.*

Another painful contraction began to swell. Large, deep inhales through her nostrils and out through her mouth helped set a soothing rhythm. Even with the pain intensifying on each contraction, she felt a confidence in her strength that had been missing during Jonathan's birth. She felt ready. Peaceful. Powerful.

Intense agony pulled her focus back to breathing and swaying. Her groans became louder. She shut the bathroom door. When a contraction subsided, she grabbed her phone and fumbled through the apps to open the contraction timer. Time seemed to be going by unusually fast, and she worried that she had lost track of the actual lengths of her contractions. *My contractions have just started. I can't be that far along.* She tried to ease her worry.

She reminded herself of all she had learned about pain, energy, and movement of anything in energy form. Her mind suddenly sprang to her knowledge of energy transfer. She remembered a documentary that had offered the theory about how the grounding of energy could be done in the mind, that grounding one's self could simply be done by envisioning a grounding source. *A powerful grounding source?* She missed Maya, who was usually there to offer good ideas.

Another contraction abruptly set in. As she swayed, she envisioned the walnut tree at a nearby park. She always marveled at its size and beauty, and she loved watching the branches sway in the breeze. *A tree!* Breathe … Sway … Breathe. As the pain slowly subsided, she thought, *The tree … A grounding source!*

At the top of the next contraction, she closed her eyes and thought about the strength of the tree and its grounding energy. With the thought of the tree, each contraction seemed to get easier and time seemed to fade away. She continued to religiously press the start and stop buttons on the contraction-tracking app while she let her mind focus on the dance she was doing to bring her baby into the world. She wanted to call her doctor, but she wondered, *Are my contractions painful enough?* She questioned her intuition, but then she remembered times in the past when she had denied her instincts and had regretted the outcomes.

She dialed her doctor's office and was told to get to the hospital despite the lack of intensity of her pain. Danyella felt a sureness in the guidance and began to prepare for her departure. The plan had always been that Jacky would accompany Danyella to the hospital thus allowing John and Jonathan to remain home. She quietly woke John and told him that Jacky was on her way to take her to the hospital. The news of his baby arriving instantly perked John's sleepy mind awake, but his excitement made it hard for her to focus on her rhythm, and the pain began to overwhelm her. She gripped his arm as she hunched over in agony and moaned through the pulsating pressure.

Watching his wife in pain, John's face flushed pink. The sound of a car pulling into their driveway brought his mind some much needed ease. Jacky had arrived. In the dark of the early morning hours, Jacky loaded Danyella and her bag into the car. John's eyes twinkled with joy as he said, "You're doing great, honey! We'll meet our baby today. I love you!"

Danyella smiled before closing her eyes and slipping into another contraction in the front seat of Jacky's car.

CHAPTER 22

DANIEL

Danyella was in between contractions when they arrived at the hospital. Anticipating the next one, she opened the car door before the tires rolled to a stop. "I'll meet you upstairs!" Danyella shouted while darting for the entrance. She made it to the door marked Labor and Delivery on the third floor before hunching over while trying to breathe and focus through another crippling contraction. A nurse saw her in pain and ran to her side. "Let's get you checked in, honey," she said while guiding her to the desk and rubbing her back.

Nurses behind the counter looked up when Danyella and the friendly nurse approached the station. Judging that Danyella was pretty close to pushing, they rushed her into a birthing room while asking Danyella all the necessary questions. Danyella feverishly changed out of her clothes and into a hospital gown.

"Do you want an epidural?" a nurse asked her as she began to set up the room. Danyella had originally planned to give birth without medication, and since she was in between waves of harsh pain, she replied, "No, thank you." But then as the pain began to intensify, she wondered if she had made the right decision.

The sight of Jacky being ushered into the birthing room brought Danyella comfort. Having her big sister by her side encouraged an unexplainable strength she knew she needed. Jacky quickly unloaded her arms full of bags and pillows and rushed to her sister's side. Danyella winced at the start of another contraction that pulled her down into a squatting position near the floor. *Splat!* Warm water gushed all around her feet. "I ... I ... I want that epidural *now!*" Danyella said as the pain became so harsh that it felt like it was strangling her.

The nurse grabbed a stack of towels and rushed to the mini pool of water around Danyella's and Jacky's feet. "I think it's too late for an epidural. Let's get you in the bed and check you," the nurse said in a calmer tone than her face revealed.

Danyella's mind was spinning. She had never before felt such intense pressure. Lifting her leg to get into the hospital bed, she felt her body start to push and bear down. She screamed, "He's coming!"

Knowing she didn't need to check, the nurse quickly called for the doctor.

Danyella panicked and began to hyperventilate. Jacky's face was the only thing Danyella could focus on. It was as if the room had fallen silent and was slowly going dark. She saw Jacky's lips moving and the excitement of others frantically moving around the room behind her in a blur.

Focus! You need to focus!

Suddenly, the sound snapped back within her ears. She took a gasping breath before shouting, "I need to focus!"

"Yes you do. You're doing great!" a woman in a white doctor's coat said while smiling at Danyella and holding one hand on her knee. Danyella's mind whirled at all the new faces in the room. The few seconds of panic had felt like several minutes someplace else. "I'm Doctor Joy. I'm the doctor onsite this morning. I'll be delivering your baby," she said, smiling. Danyella nodded and braced for the uptick in pain.

Like a soldier focusing on an upcoming battle, Danyella cleared her mind to give all her physical strength to this one moment. "Push! Push! Push!" a chorus of female voices shouted. And Danyella pushed. She pushed again and again until she heard Dr. Joy shout, "Reach down and grab your baby!" Danyella's nervous hands did what she was told. As her hands grasped the tiny, wet body, she felt a rush of energy that she knew all too well. Her jaw dropped as she pulled baby Daniel up to her chest. Her tears started to stream. Her heart felt full. The only words of gratitude she could muster in a whisper to her crying baby were, "Hi, Maya!"

Many tears, stitches, and minutes later, Danyella watched her long-awaited baby sleep in her arms. As her eyes soaked in the perfection of her child, she thought about the times Maya had guided her from heaven. Maya's instructions on how Danyella would know that she had arrived on earth became crystal clear. She had been right. Danyella had undeniably felt Maya's energy at the first touch of baby Daniel. There was no doubt in her mind that she was finally here. She remembered Maya saying, *If you doubt yourself, look for Joy.* "Of course I'd be full of joy with you arriving, you little trickster!" Danyella whispered as she snuggled her baby close.

A smiling doctor came in to check on mom and baby. "How are things going, Mom?"

"We're doing just great!"

"I wanted to tell you how wonderful you did this morning!"

Danyella blushed at the thought of her hyperventilating during birth being wonderful . "Thanks."

"When I first arrived, you seemed to be in doubt, and I thought it might be that you had been worried I wouldn't get here in time for this little guy's arrival, but you quickly kicked into gear and pulled yourself back. You were amazing! I'm glad I could assist you. Congrats!"

"I'm so thankful you were there too, Dr. Joy," Danyella said while smiling at baby Daniel.

"Oh my gosh!" Dr. Joy gasped. "It looks like he's already trying to smile." She leaned over to hug Danyella, who felt that Dr. Joy was an earthly angel sent to remind Danyella of her strength in truth. Maya had been right. Joy was in the room, in more ways than one.

John and Jonathan walked into the room just when Danyella was beginning to miss them. Jonathan seemed a year older to Danyella after holding her small baby, Daniel, all morning. John's eyes glossed over with happy tears as he approached his wife and newborn son. Jonathan clung to his dad's shoulder tightly in nervousness of the new situation.

"Oh, honey! He's so beautiful!" John said.

"Daddy and Jonathan, meet our Daniel." The words *our Daniel* sounded perfect.

While holding his new baby, John looked at Danyella with a twinkle in his eye and said, "Born on three nineteen! I thought for sure he was waiting to arrive on your special day, the twenty-second." It was John's way of expressing his belief in Danyella's relationship with their son, a peace offering of sorts.

Danyella smiled. "It wouldn't be like him to come on a day that I had expected or in a way I'd expected."

They laughed while smiling at baby Daniel, who was bundled up tight and fast asleep. Just then, Danyella was struck with the sum of three and nineteen. *I guess you did come on a day of twenty-two after all, huh, baby Daniel? I'll keep that our little secret for now.*

The family of four huddled together in awe and admiration of their newest member. And once again, for Danyella, time was lost.

The next day, Danyella and Daniel were discharged and happily went home to their two Johns. She had never felt happier. Life with baby Daniel seemed more fitting than she had imagined. Her worries about little Jonathan accepting the new baby were easily wiped clean as she saw his curiosity and excitement for his little brother. With each new day that passed, the family began to find the rhythm in their new life.

It wasn't until a few months along that Danyella started to mourn Maya's missing voice. With Maya living on earth as baby Daniel, Danyella's communication with the other world was much quieter than she was used to. She missed the persistent pulls into uninvited conversations, the demands to do things a specific way, and the constant, loving energy Danyella always felt when Maya was focusing on her.

While feeding Daniel one afternoon, she said, "So now that you're here, who am I going to talk to?" Daniel looked at her with wide eyes as if he wanted to say something. Danyella was startled by a soft tickle on her arm. She looked down, saw a ladybug, and blushed. "Hi, Sofia!"